Come, My Pet

By

Keira Michelle Telford

www.venaticpress.com

PROLOGUE

As THE SUN SETS OVER THE HORIZON, THE ENGLISH countryside descends into shades of blue and gray, the pearly moon rising into the darkening sky. Naked branches of winter-stripped trees stretch their skeletal fingers up toward the emerging stars, trying to capture them in their bony grip, and frost settles on the ground, glistening in the starlight.

In the back of a limo that's winding its way along a single-lane road between the fields and pastures, cutting through patches of woodland, twenty-eight-year-old Coralie slouches on the leather upholstery, staring at the passing wilderness.

Her long raven curls tumble over her shoulders, silky and smooth, shimmering with a blue hue cast upon her through the limo's moon-roof. She's wearing one of her best outfits—an ankle-length red satin skirt with a black lace-up bodice—and as she crosses her legs, the skirt glides over her knee, a side slit baring her slender, stockinged legs. In that moment, the eyes that'd been riveted to the upper swells of her generous breasts for most of the journey drop swiftly to her thighs.

She's aware of the attention but pretends otherwise. The delicious young woman eyeballing her from the seat opposite is Bink, her aunt Alessa's life companion, and her gussied-up aunt—also dressed in her finest eveningwear—is right there, watching everything.

Older than Coralie, Alessa is in her early fifties, her once jet black hair now invaded with flecks of silver. Angered by Bink's wandering interest, she clenches her jaw, her fist tightening around a chain clutched in her hand.

"That's my niece you're gawping at!" She finally snaps, slapping Bink across the head. "Show some respect!"

The other end of the chain is clipped to a wide black leather collar buckled around Bink's neck, and as Bink—a boyish blonde in black jeans, a white shirt, and a charcoal gray waistcoat—cowers in anticipation of further rebuke, Alessa jerks her to the floor of the limo, wrenching her by the chain.

When she's down on her hands and knees, Alessa snatches a riding crop off the seat and cracks it across her back. Once. Twice. Three times. Bink holds back a shriek of pain and squeezes her eyes shut, her silent tears dripping onto the floor.

"Stop!" Coralie lunges forward and grabs the whip before the fourth strike, wresting it out of Alessa's grasp. "That's enough! You're hurting her!"

"That's the point." Alessa slumps back into her seat. "Companions are like dogs: they need to be taught their place. When you finally have one of your own, you'll understand."

"I doubt that." Coralie keeps hold of the whip. "You think the only way to command respect is through pain and punishment? You're wrong." She tosses the whip into the back of the limo, far out of Alessa's reach. "No dog should fear its Mistress." She watches Bink huddle on the floor, curled into a tight ball. "And no companion should, either."

Alessa laughs cruelly. "You're soft."

"You're cold," Coralie retorts. "A companion will do anything for the love of her Mistress, but you'll never appreciate that. All any creature needs is love, and the bond between a companion and her Mistress should be stronger than any other."

Alessa snorts. "Love? What do you know about love? You'll fuck anything with tits and you've never loved a thing in your life."

Coralie bites her tongue, turning away from Alessa as the limo pulls up in the driveway of a large stone manor house: their destination for the weekend. This conversation can wait.

Stepping out of the vehicle, she follows her aunt and Bink into the manor's grand entrance hall, where a gaggle of other women are already congregated. *Introitus: Requiem Aeternum*, the first movement in Mozart's *Requiem*, plays unobtrusively in the background, its soothing and familiar notes barely audible above all the chatter. The air is heavy. It smells like lilac and primrose, mixed with the faint but discernible odor of burning apple tree bark, and a trace of elecampagne, hung in small sheaves above the doorways.

Attendants of this exclusive monthly event are split into two groups: the Mistresses of the High Council—of which Alessa is one—and junior Mistresses, like Coralie. All the High Council members are accompanied by their silent and uniformly-dressed companions, but the juniors must attend alone. They won't get to claim companions of their own until they have the privilege of ascending to the High Council.

It's a coveted bond, yet the loyal young companions are, for the most part, barely acknowledged. They're made to stand a pace or two behind their hardhearted Mistresses, collared and chained, tethered to them at all times. The highlight of their evening is occasionally being dragged from one place to another to be ignored some more.

They don't get to drink the complimentary champagne, nor even appreciate their lavish surroundings. And this place *is* lavish. The curtains are red velvet with saffron-colored tiebacks, gold thread woven throughout, and the stairs are carpeted with the same. Every bit of furniture is antique, in pristine condition, preserved from generation to generation, and the walls are covered with ornately-framed portraits.

In the entrance hall, the portraits are those of former High Council members who were privileged enough to sit at the head of the council table. In the richly decorated front room, a large portrait of Hecate, the goddess of witchcraft, dominates the wall above the fireplace, surrounded by brass reliefs of the Lampades: the torch-bearing nymphs said to accompany the goddess on her travels.

Elsewhere, more chthonic deities are given wall space: Persephone, Queen of the underworld; Nyx, the goddess of night; Melinoë, the goddess of ghosts; and Macaria, the goddess of blessed death.

Coralie swipes a glass of champagne off a table at the center of the room and makes a halfhearted effort to mingle with the other members of her coven. All the while, Bink steals surreptitious glances at her, trying to be discreet, but failing to hide a blush as certain aspects of her anatomy respond all too readily to Coralie's womanly form.

And Coralie can't help but be aroused by the interest. She once saw Bink naked, straight out of a hot bath, her snowy skin pink and glowing. She ought to have looked away, but Bink's body was entrancing. Her surprisingly full breasts jutted out proudly from her chest, ornamented with hardened ruby tips. How she wanted to wrap her lips around those swollen nipples ... but that would've been a gross violation of coven law.

No Mistress can enjoy another's companion without express consent, and Alessa's never been the sharing type. Working her way through the room, Coralie sidles up behind Bink, taking care to stay out of her austere aunt's sightline.

"Are you all right, my lovely?" she whispers in Bink's ear. "I hope Mistress Alessa didn't hurt you too badly when she punished you for ogling me in the car."

Bink cannot speak without direct permission from her Mistress, so she says nothing, shivering as Coralie runs a hand down her whip-lashed back, making her flesh tingle. They may not be permitted to touch intimately, but Coralie is an expert at skirting the thin line of propriety.

"Next time, make sure you don't get caught." She pats Bink on the bum, downs the rest of her champagne, and moves away, her attention drawn to one of the other junior Mistresses.

Eighteen-year-old Liora is the youngest, newest member of the coven, and Coralie wasted no time introducing herself to the freckled redhead at the last gathering. Traditionally, freshly initiated junior Mistresses give the first of themselves to one of the many unbonded companions in the coterie: a private room at the back of the manor where all the available playmates are kept for their exclusive pleasure. But Liora never got the chance for that. Coralie seduced her, and had the first of her on the High Council's dining room table.

"Good evening, my darling." Coralie sweeps a hand around Liora's slender waist and maneuvers her into a quiet corner, shoving her against the wall and pinning her there. "Shall we retire to the coterie and have some fun together?"

Liora giggles, weak to Coralie's sexual force. "You've only been here five minutes."

"That's five arduous minutes I've endured without tasting your sweet cunt." Coralie takes her by the hand and drags her out of the front room. "Let's not waste any more."

Honestly, there's little else for them to do. In a few minutes, the High Council members will sequester themselves in their private chamber for hours on end, while the junior Mistresses are excluded from the proceedings on account of their inferior status.

As they breeze into the hallway, several other junior Mistresses follow in their wake. The door to the coterie is at the end of the hall, and along the way, they pass the open door to the High Council's private dining room, the sight of it stirring a flicker of envy in Coralie's chest.

The table is set for dinner, an assortment of black and red candles arranged in the centerpieces, ready to be lit. Open fires are burning at either end of the room, the logs crackling and hissing. Around the table, twenty-two chairs are spaced wide enough to accommodate large red velvet cushions on the floor beside each, providing a place for the companions to sit at their Mistresses' feet.

Coralie couldn't care less about the food they're going to serve, but she wants a seat at the table. She's hungry for it. She wants influence over the coven, she wants a companion of her own, and more than anything, she wants a child. Only members of the High Council are allowed to conceive, and she can feel her best child-bearing years slipping away.

"Stop drooling," Liora teases, too young to truly understand her desperation.

"You don't know what it's like," Coralie grumbles, sweeping a hand across her abdomen. "I'm twenty-eight years old already. How much longer am I expected to wait? I'm fertile and I want to bear children."

"You're next in line." Liora tries to brighten her suddenly soured mood. "Your aunt sits on the Council and she's past breeding age. Maybe she'll relinquish her position?"

"As if." Coralie sighs. "They're all too enamored with the prestige of running the coven. The only way to ascend these days is when one of them dies, and those old crones live forever."

Subdued by her impatience, but determined to make the best of what she has, she takes a deep, restorative breath and strides into the coterie, inhaling the familiar aroma of sex and scented lubricants.

The long room is lined with alcoves, each one just big enough to snugly accommodate a double bed. If privacy is required, a net curtain can be pulled across the alcove, somewhat obscuring it from prying eyes—not that Coralie's ever been bothered by an audience. Behind three of these closed curtains, a handful of junior Mistresses are already partaking in the abundant delights of the many playmates, but there's plenty more to go around.

Outside each unoccupied alcove, a playmate sits tethered to the wall, waiting to please. Naked except for the leather collars around their necks, they exist only to provide physical pleasure to the junior Mistresses as and when required.

Selected for their agreeable features and fine figures, they're perfect examples of the female form in every way. At least, they were until they were initiated into the coterie. Now, they all have a certain physical enhancement, and Coralie's focus is diverted from Liora as a well-proportioned blonde waiting patiently to be of use rises onto all fours and dips her head, bowing reverently as she presents herself for the choosing, her nipples stiff, her big cock—her priapus—swinging between her legs.

"Fawn." Coralie smiles at the subservient playmate. "I've missed you."

Though she'd find the distinctly male organ utterly repulsive if it were attached to a hard, masculine body, seeing it protruding from Fawn's nethers has a profoundly different effect. Aching to be touched, she releases Fawn from the tether, flops onto the bed, and parts her legs, promising Liora a tongue-lashing as soon as her more imminent needs are sated.

"Have you missed me, darling?" She flips her skirt to the side, unveiling her naked sex.

Fawn nods, kissing her ankle, purring softly.

"Then show me." Coralie spreads her legs wider, inviting Fawn to devour her.

Dutifully, the playmate responds to her need and edges forward, working kisses upward to her deprived core and eliciting a voluptuous moan when she engages mouth and fingers simultaneously, slipping two digits inside while sucking on Coralie's swollen clit.

"That's it," Coralie whimpers. "I need you."

Without fail, the sex between them is passionate, lustful, and energetic, but while relationships in the coterie are often intense, they're far from exclusive. Fawn will tend to other junior Mistresses upon their request, and Coralie will not limit her pleasure. Indeed, Coralie has been known to take five or six playmates at once, making thorough good use of each one as well as several other junior Mistresses. Even those who only lick and suck are rendered limp and exhausted by the time she's done with them.

Of course, it's the ultimate desire of all playmates to one day become the bonded companion of a Mistress of the High Council. For that reason, most use their time in the coterie to attach themselves to a particular junior Mistress, hoping that she'll reward their eagerness by choosing to form a permanent bond with them when she finally ascends.

In this pursuit, Fawn is no exception. She's been trying to ingratiate herself with Coralie for years, and while she's clearly the forerunner in Coralie's affections, and would dearly love to have a monopoly on providing her sexual gratification, she's unable to voice any complaint when the prurient Mistress spies two other playmates creeping toward the alcove and invites them to join in.

"Darlings." She welcomes them onto the bed.

They work together to unlace her bodice, taking one breast each, and she lets out another deep moan. The attention of Fawn's mouth and fingers coupled with their tender ministrations soon has her on the cusp of a volcanic orgasm, and she cries out as her paroxysm begins to crest, her whole body quivering, her cunt pulsing and throbbing. In the wake of it, she peers down, staring at Fawn's fully engorged augmentation.

"My dearest Fawn." She groans, admiring her favorite playmate's virility. "I wish we could enjoy that beautiful body of yours to its full potential." She strokes her fingers over Fawn's flushed cheeks. "You'd give me a baby, wouldn't you? If only my aunt weren't in the way."

Fawn nuzzles Coralie's flat belly, more than willing to lay claim on her reproductive future.

"I know you would." Coralie weaves her fingers through Fawn's golden mane. "In the meantime, fuck me well."

Without hesitation, Fawn slides her hands around Coralie's rump, raises her off the bed, and drives all the way into her, filling her on the first plunge. Using all her strength, she pulls Coralie down to meet every thrust, slamming into her over and over again. Trained well, she won't reach her peak until Coralie asks for it, no matter how long she's made to wait.

Five minutes.

Ten.

Twenty.

Then ...

"Come for me, Fawn," Coralie mewls, visualizing Fawn's potent libation erupting into her womb, longing for the day when she'll finally be able to conceive.

Part One

Bonding

CHAPTER ONE

One month later ...

THE FIRST TIME CORALIE STEPS INSIDE THE GRAND DINING room reserved exclusively for the High Council, she feels a swell of pride. She's been prepared for this moment her whole adult life, and it's been far too long in coming.

For her introduction, she's brought in alongside the current head of the council, Mistress Diana, who rose to her place at the top simply by bearing the most offspring. Though her fertile years are now well behind her, no Mistress at the table has yet surpassed her, so her position remains unchallenged.

As the other Mistresses take their seats, Diana presents Coralie to them with a thin-lipped smile, her silvery ball gown matching the color of her shoulder-length hair and the diamonds around her neck.

"Tonight, ladies, we welcome a new High Council member to the table." She initiates a small round of applause. "Mistress Coralie replaces our good friend Mistress Alessa, who unfortunately is no longer with us."

"So sorry about your aunt, dear." One of the Mistresses near the head of the table shakes her head despondently, mourning the loss of a colleague. "Such a terrible, unfortunate thing to have fallen down all those stairs at the last gathering."

"Yes, it was a tragic accident," Coralie concurs dispassionately.

Waiting for no further invitation, she takes it upon herself to sit in the only vacant chair, opposite a Mistress several years her senior. With yellowy-gray hair and a few lines on her face, Mistress Isabelle is nudging up against fifty years of age. A heavy drinker with a short temper and a penchant for sadism, Coralie knows of her via coterie gossip, though they've never officially met.

As she settles into her seat, she's watched intently by a brunette sitting on the floor to Mistress Isabelle's left. Noting the interest from the young companion, and welcoming it, Coralie flashes her a smile.

Taken aback to be acknowledged so casually, when it's the general practice of the Mistresses to behave as though any companions other than their own are virtual non-entities, the demure brunette blushes furiously and averts her gaze. In so doing, she inadvertently rattles the heavy chain fixed to her leather collar, drawing Isabelle's attention to her.

"Sit still, Pet!" Isabelle jerks on the chain, yanking the brunette closer.

Though all companions are tethered, most are not treated so harshly. Pet's alabaster skin is marked with purple bruises around her collar, indicative of her having been repeatedly pulled this way and that, the discomfort used as a form of correction for unwanted behaviors.

Coralie is unimpressed. According to the gossip mongers, Isabelle, upon nearing the end of her childbearing years and seeking to move further up in the ranks before the chance escaped her altogether, severed her permanent bond with her former—supposedly underperforming—companion. To achieve that, she tricked her sweet, trusting mate into committing a violation of coven law, thus resulting in her collar being stripped. Believing that she could harness much more potent seed in a younger specimen, she then claimed Pet at the tender age of eighteen, snapping her up before anyone else got a look in.

That was a little over six months ago.

Still no pregnancy.

Coralie—in her reproductive prime, thank the gods—can't help but feel sorry for Pet. Companions are hardwired to procreate. Their sole purpose in life is to be bonded to a Mistress and fill her fertile womb, and Pet has the misfortune of being trapped with an older woman whose capacity to breed has already ebbed by.

It's such a terrible waste, Coralie thinks, pressing a hand to her aching abdomen, the burning need to further her own bloodline growing ever more demanding. Pet cannot break her bond, and having engineered the expulsion of one companion already, neither can Isabelle. She dare not, lest her dubious actions should be called into question.

Looking around the table, Coralie observes the other Mistresses with their companions, watching how they offer food to their tethered mates at intervals. Most opt to hand-feed, this simple act strengthening the bond between them, but Pet's dinner plate is conspicuously empty. She's offered nothing. Not a single morsel.

Coralie catches her ogling some of the tabletop treats, her hunger evident. This time, Pet meets her gaze and doesn't look away, fixing her bright eyes—one blue, one amber—on Coralie's deep emeralds.

In a trait common to all bonded companions, Pet's eyes are burning with such an intensity that they appear iridescent, shimmering continuously, and Coralie feels a small prick of jealousy. By any standards, Pet's beautiful. She has a long, naturally wavy mane of thick, reddy-brown hair falling loose over her shoulders, her straight-cut bangs—much too long and in need of a trim—parted in the middle and draped around her eyes.

Delightfully petite, she'd be lucky to stretch on her tippy toes to reach much over five feet, and as suits her waif-like figure, her breasts are small and firm. Having no need to wear a bra, both unfettered mounds tent out her white button-up shirt, two dark pink circles hinting at the presence of her areolae beyond the thin cotton.

Feeling her own nipples harden in response to her scrutiny of Pet's body, Coralie glides a hand from her neckline to her waist, pretending to smooth out creases in her bodice, giving one of her breasts a surreptitious squeeze along the way.

Pet's jaw slackens, her eyes locked on Coralie's ample bosom, shocked but thrilled by the display, which she can only imagine must be for her benefit.

"Cover yourself up!" Isabelle barks then, though not at Coralie and her protruding nipples, but at Pet. "How many times must I tell you?" She slaps her hand across Pet's forehead, roughly smoothing out her bangs. "No-one ever knows which one to look at." She conceals Pet's unusual eyes behind her reddish locks. "It's confusing."

Obediently, Pet sits still, waiting until her Mistress is suitably distracted by another glass of specially selected wine before she tilts her head sideways, causing her bangs to part around her blue eye, allowing her to peer up at Coralie once more.

She's rewarded with the warmest of smiles, making her heart flutter.

Picking up on Coralie's interest, one of the Mistresses seated beside her tries to strike up a conversation about what type of companion she might be interested in claiming for herself now that her time has come.

"What's your taste?" the nosey Mistress pries, expecting a standard answer emphasizing the length and girth of her preferred companion's augmentation.

"My taste?" Coralie's eyes drift back to Pet. "Young. Dark hair. Pretty eyes."

Not used to such attention—or compliments of any kind, no matter how indirect—Pet's cheeks burn. Self-conscious, she looks away, turning her head to obscure the flush of color, her movement accidentally pulling the chain taut and jolting Isabelle out of a half-sleep.

"Get down, Pet!" The drunken Mistress pushes on Pet's head, shoving her to the floor.

Refusing to let that be an end to their flirtation—in fact, seeing this as an opportunity to further it—Coralie tucks her chair closer to the table and uncrosses her legs. While continuing to pick at her dinner, she slips her free hand beneath the table and onto her lap. Pinching her ankle-length skirt between her fingers, she tugs it up inch by inch, baring her legs by increments until she succeeds in getting the hem above her knees. Then, she waits.

The faint jangle of Pet's chain signals the affection-starved companion edging forward, inching her way beneath the table, repositioning herself for a better look.

Indeed, in the dim, narrow passage littered with crumbs and dropped napkins, the long tablecloth concealing all sins, Pet cranes her neck, hoping for even the briefest glimpse of the forbidden treasure hiding at the top of Coralie's long, stockinged legs.

As if sensing that silent pleading, Coralie shifts in her chair. Angling her hips forward, she grabs the bunched up hem in her fist and pulls it up her thighs, simultaneously parting her legs.

Pet can smell her arousal. Stifling a surprised whimper as her own arousal causes her priapus to stiffen, she looks down at her crotch, the thick appendage clearly visible, the bulbous head pinched between the waistband of her jeans and her stomach. It hurts.

Stuffing her hand inside her clothing, she makes a quick adjustment, forcing her rigid shaft down her pant leg instead, giving it more room and allowing it to grow to full hardness against her thigh. It's still uncomfortable, but at least it's not painful.

Eagerly returning to Coralie's display, she watches as the unbonded Mistress strokes her inner thigh, dragging her blood red fingernails over the pale flesh above her stocking, moving toward a thick thatch of dark hair at her core.

Pet wriggles nearer. Lowering her head, she presses her lips to the toe of one of Coralie's red patent leather stilettos, dropping a single kiss there, demonstrating her appreciation in the only way she can. Feeling brave in that moment, and intoxicated with lust, she wraps her hands around Coralie's slender foot, planting kisses all over, working her way up from foot to ankle to calf and shin, not daring to venture above the knee. That would be too intimate. Too improper.

Closer now, Coralie's scent is overwhelming. Her pubic hair is glistening with moisture, and Pet's breath catches in her throat as Coralie trails an adventurous hand toward that black triangle, her pink concealed by the hair surrounding it.

Overcome with want, she shuffles between Coralie's legs. Her shoulders nudge Coralie's knees, forcing her to spread open wider, and Coralie struggles not to give them both away, her excitement heightened by Pet's unexpected enthusiasm.

Controlling her breathing as best she can, Coralie slips her pale fingers into her tangle of damp curls and glides downward. When she reaches her labia, she uses her fore and ring fingers to spread her lips, then dips her middle finger into her heat.

For almost a full minute, she probes her slit, languidly fucking herself, making sure her finger is slick with her honey before she withdraws and extends her hand, offering the sticky digit to Pet's mouth.

At great risk of spontaneously ejaculating, Pet closes her eyes, purrs, and breathes in Coralie's unique perfume. Tableside, Coralie feels Pet's warm breath on her hand. She waits to feel the hot lash of an eager tongue, but as Pet's lips part and the very tip of her tongue makes contact, the chain clanks, alerting Isabelle to her movements.

"What're you doing down there?!" Isabelle wrenches Pet back into place.

As the thick leather collar crushes Pet's throat, Pet yelps, her cry of pain met with an open-palm smack to the back of her head.

"Is that really necessary?" Coralie targets the inebriated Mistress with a stern glare. "She didn't do anything wrong."

Isabelle reaches for her glass, glancing at the empty space beside Coralie. "Where's your companion? Oh, that's right: you don't have one." She downs half the glass in one gulp. "Perhaps you should reserve your criticism for a topic you actually know something about. Fucking, maybe. That is what you do best, isn't it?"

One of the other Mistresses, having briefly witnessed Coralie's antics in the coterie before her own ascension to the High Council, snorts and laughs. "Is there any playmate you haven't sampled? I've seen you go through six in one night!"

"There's no harm in enjoying oneself." Coralie smiles wickedly, winking at Pet when Isabelle isn't looking.

"Maybe so, but the time for such dalliances has now passed," the Mistress reminds her. "Do you think it possible for you to be content with just one companion? Given your history, a monogamous relationship might prove to be somewhat ... tame."

"I don't envisage that being a problem." Coralie's gaze drifts back to Pet, finding her head angled forward, her bangs flopped in front of her face, concealing her flaming cheeks.

"Well, you'll get to hook your claws into one after dinner." The unaware Mistress digs at her food, oblivious to the flirtation going on in front of her. "Mistress Diana has a whole swathe of eligible playmates for you to pick through, but perhaps you already have a favorite from your time spent in the coterie?"

"I can't say that I do." Coralie keeps her eyes on Pet. "Not anymore."

CHAPTER TWO

CORALIE LOUNGES ON A PURPLE VELVET CHAISE IN THE drawing room, sipping champagne. She's been told to sit back and enjoy the view as a string of potential companions are paraded in front of her for her choosing, but the exhibition is becoming repetitive.

First five, then ten, then fifteen. Some are playmates familiar to her from the coterie, while others are fresh faces, virginal and recently initiated into the coven.

As one Mistress leads another handful of rejects out into the hall, banishing them back to their domain in the coterie, Mistress Diana ushers in five more topless prospects, instructing them to form a neat line in front of Coralie. Of this batch, she recognizes only one: Fawn.

Though Fawn attempts to make eye contact, Coralie remains aloof, giving no indication as to their acquaintance, nor that she has any intention of choosing Fawn to be her companion. And so the selection process continues.

"Bare," Diana points a riding crop at the prospect on the far left.

Without protest, the tall blonde unbuckles her black jeans, tugs them off her hips, and exposes her flaccid priapus. In its current state, it resembles a tiny grub worm.

A few seconds later, Diana issues the same command to the next in line. This prospect's cheeks burn as she pulls down her pants, revealing her semi-erect augmentation. It fattens more under the attention of Coralie's eyes, but doesn't reach much more than five inches.

The third prospect, Fawn, has more to be proud of—as Coralie well knows. When she unzips herself, her bulky, rock hard priapus flops out, bobbing in front of her, but Coralie simply signals to Diana to move on down the line, having numbers four and five bare themselves simultaneously, her casual disinterest inflaming a quietly seething anger behind Fawn's eyes.

Oblivious to that, and thoroughly bored by these proceedings, Coralie's mind drifts and she thinks about Pet. None of the prospects she's seen thus far have sparked even half as much desire in her, and as the evening drags on, the only thing growing is her ennui.

"Could we take a break?" She smothers a yawn, preventing Diana from wrangling together yet another set of hopefuls. "This is getting dreadfully tiresome."

"Do you not like any of them?" Diana sighs, planting a hand on her hip. "I don't know what more you expect. Tall, short, blonde, brunette—you've seen it all."

"And they're all fine enough." Coralie gets up. "But I have to visit the little girls' room."

Excusing herself to the other Mistresses, she slinks out of the drawing room, stumbling upon a sour-looking Pet sitting cross-legged on the hallway floor, tethered to a railing outside the washroom. Slouched over, her elbows are propped on her knees, her chin cupped in the heels of her palms. She's exuding misery.

"Pet?" Coralie approaches her. "What's wrong?"

Caught unawares, Pet bolts upright, trying to compose herself. The hallway is lined with chairs on which the playmates and new initiates were told to sit and wait before being led five or six at a time into the drawing room, and Pet's spent a significant amount of time feeling sorry for herself, her heart sinking minute by minute.

"Why are you sad?" Coralie settles into the chair nearest to her.

Incapable of lying to a Mistress—*any* Mistress—Pet tips her head in the direction of the drawing room, then quickly turns away, painfully aware that she has no right to express any feelings on the matter.

"Are you jealous?" Coralie infers from her behavior. "You think I'm in there pawing on a roomful of potential mates, drooling over their delicious bodies?"

Under the guise of fixing an imperfection with one of her stockings, she uncrosses her legs, flicks her skirt over her knees, and bends forward, trailing a pale, slender hand from her ankle to her thigh, grazing her fingernails along the silky fabric.

"The truth is," she goes on, "I've been very much distracted."

Pet is captivated. She follows the path of Coralie's hand, watching it linger on her upper thigh as she fingers the lacy elastic at the top of the stocking, stroking her palm over the smooth, pale skin above.

"You see, sweet Pet"—Coralie crosses her legs again, making no attempt to cover back up, leaving herself indecently exposed—"I can't stop thinking about this adorable young thing I met at dinner." She grips Pet's cheeks, demanding her whole and undivided attention. "She's perfect in every way, and she excites me beyond all good reason, even though she belongs to another." Her eyes drop to Pet's lap, pleased to find her fully erect.

Uneasy with such close contact in such an open place, and terrified that Mistress Isabelle will return from the washroom to catch her aroused and flirting with someone else, Pet wrests her head away from Coralie's clutches, turning her face to hide her shame.

"Has she been gone long?" Coralie interprets her concern.

Pet nods.

Without further word, Coralie rises from the chair and enters the washroom to investigate, coming upon Isabelle passed out on the marble floor. She's curled around the base of the toilet, vomit everywhere, her skirt scrunched up and her knickers bared, a full bush of graying pubic hair peeking out around the edges.

Disgusted, Coralie kicks the old drunkard's shin with the pointed toe of her stiletto, testing to see how likely she is to be roused. The answer? Not very. Isabelle grunts and snorts, but remains unconscious.

Swinging open the washroom door, Coralie beckons to an obediently waiting Pet. "Come, Pet." She unclips the companion from her chain. "Come see your Mistress."

Pet stands, but takes no step forward. She brings a hand to her neck, looping a finger through the brass ring where her chain is always fixed, her eyes pinned to the links of heavy steel now dangling limply from the railing.

Coralie hooks a finger under her chin, tilting her head up. "Are you going to run away from me, Pet?"

Pet locks onto Coralie's emerald eyes, giving her head a small shake.

"Then what do we need it for?" Coralie beams. "Come." She takes Pet by the hand and leads her into the washroom, directing her to the corner in which Isabelle is slumped.

"Here she is in all her glory." Coralie folds her arms, glaring disdainfully at the pitiful, graceless, aging witch.

Mortified on her Mistress's behalf, Pet lowers her gaze, not wanting to look. Tears prick her eyes, but she holds them back, gasping when Coralie's warm hands reach for her again, this time lightly cupping her face.

"I'm sorry she hurt you at dinner." Coralie thumbs the young companion's peachy cheeks. "That was my fault."

Pet shakes her head, halfheartedly shrugging one shoulder: It's no big deal. She expects Coralie to withdraw, and instinctively flinches when Coralie's hands slip down to her bruised neck.

"Let me," Coralie insists, reaching out to her again. "Let me kiss it better."

Torn between obedience to this new, dangerously alluring Mistress and loyalty to the pathetic scrap of a woman she's bonded to, Pet closes her eyes and relents, allowing Coralie to angle her head back, baring her neck.

"Good, Pet," Coralie whispers, bringing her soft mouth to the damaged skin on Pet's throat, above her collar. "I'll make it all go away."

Pet mewls as Coralie's hands slide around her neck, holding her in place, adorning her with kisses, and her skin tingles where Coralie's lips grace her, the pain dulled. The pain ... gone. Pet opens her eyes and peeks at her reflection in the washroom mirror, finding the skin around her collar pale and flawless, the bruises vanished.

"I told you." Coralie smiles warmly, admiring her handiwork. "Now, if you'll permit me to do so, I'd like to finish what we started at the dinner table."

Pet cocks her head, her brow furrowed.

"I want to give you a little of what you never got to taste." Coralie moves toward to the granite counter and tugs up the hem of her skirt, holding it mid-thigh.

Realizing what she has in mind, Pet's breathing quickens. Her anxiety apparent, she backs up a half-step and bumps into a wall, her retreat impeded.

"Don't you want to?" Coralie loosens her grip on the satin, as if to drop it ...

On impulse, Pet lunges forward, placing her hand over Coralie's, preventing her from letting go. Immediately shocked by her own behavior, she then recoils, stuffing both hands in her pockets, her head dipped meekly. She ought never to touch a Mistress unless invited to do so. She ought not to be here at all, and yet ... she's salivating, her priapus twitching inside her clothes, and she can't tear her eyes away from the treasure hiding at the apex of Coralie's thighs.

"It's okay." Coralie lifts herself up onto the counter. "I won't ask you to break any of your vows. I just want you to watch. Like you did before."

She bunches her skirt around her hips, exposing that lush, full mound of dark hair at her core, and tickles her fingers around her hidden clit.

Within seconds, Pet's erection—which had withered only slightly since Coralie's display in the hall—is back at full force, straining inside her pants. Feeling a droplet of excitement ooze from the tip and dribble down her thigh, she groans.

"Come closer, Pet," Coralie begs huskily. "I promise I won't touch you."

Pet obeys, albeit hesitantly, entranced by the action of Coralie's fingers. When she's near enough, Coralie places one foot on her shoulder and leans back against the wall, opening herself up, giving Pet an enhanced view.

"Oh, Pet." She probes herself vigorously, knowing that Pet's attention is glued to her carmine slit. "I wish you could feel how wet you make me."

She begins to shake.

Feeling the pre-orgasmic tension in her body, Pet pulls her hands out of her pockets and clasps Coralie's ankle, stroking and rubbing it, her gentle touch enough to send the misbehaving Mistress over the edge.

"Do you want me to come for you?" Coralie inadvertently digs her stiletto heel into Pet's shoulder, her body shuddering, her cunt clenching around her fingers. "Tell me! Quick!"

Pet whimpers, nodding fervently.

"Oh, darling! Yes!" Coralie wails at the ceiling, the moment of crisis upon her.

For a full minute thereafter, she doesn't move, her body limp, her head spinning. All the while, Pet continues to caress her ankle and calf—the few parts of her she feels comfortable groping—and purrs softly, vocalizing her pleasure in the only way she can.

When she's suitably recovered, Coralie slides her foot off Pet's shoulder and sits up, easing her fingers out of her lubricious channel. "For you, my sweet." She runs the tip of her index finger over Pet's lips, painting her with a sheen of sex gloss.

On the brink of ejaculation once again, Pet hesitates and looks back at Isabelle. It isn't proper for a bonded companion to be hand-fed by anyone other than her Mistress, but ... this isn't food, is it? Torn between lust and propriety, she dithers, her lips trembling.

"It's all right." Coralie tiptoes her fingertips into Pet's mouth. "I won't tell."

Weak to the temptation, as she was underneath the dinner table, Pet succumbs. She wraps her lips around Coralie's fingers and sucks them clean, swirling her tongue around the sticky digits, relishing her first forbidden taste of Coralie's womanhood. A moment later, she feels a spontaneous burst of heat just south of her crotch, her swollen priapus spewing a torrent of hot cream into her pants.

Blushing ferociously, she releases Coralie's fingers and attempts to cover herself. Still spurting, she looks down at her unruly augmentation, silently cursing it for its lack of control as the viscous fluid seeps through the fabric of her jeans.

"Oh, darling." Coralie follows the direction of her gaze, thrilled by the sheer amount of ejaculate she's able to produce. "I'm so glad you enjoyed this as much as I did."

Pet's brow creases and she whines, distressed by the obviousness of her condition, afraid that her Mistress will wake and see her covered in her own seminal fluid—her precious milt.

"No need to fret." Coralie hops down off the counter and straightens her dress. "Go upstairs and clean yourself."

Pet shakes her head violently, jabbing her finger in the direction of her Mistress.

"Do as I say," Coralie insists firmly, but with a reassuring smile. "Mistress Isabelle is in no condition to give you instruction. If anyone questions your whereabouts, I shall take the blame. But go now."

Struck by the authority in Coralie's voice, Pet does as she's told. As soon as she's gone, Coralie's smile drops, a scowl taking its place. She strides over to Isabelle, grabs a fistful of her hair, and heaves her up from the floor. Demonstrating an unlikely amount of strength, she pulls the now gurgling, mumbling Mistress across the room and throws her over the counter, smacking her head on the granite.

"Wake up," she growls, shoving Isabelle's face into the porcelain basin and turning on the faucet, spraying her face with cold water.

Isabelle regains some semblance of consciousness and tries to fight Coralie off, coughing and sputtering, but Coralie is a good deal stronger and keeps her pinned.

"You're a disgrace!" Coralie looms over her. "Pet deserves better."

With that, she throws Isabelle to the floor and walks out, the stench of sex lingering in the air.

CHAPTER THREE

CORALIE LIES AWAKE, THE NIGHT MOVING INTO THE WEE hours of the morning. Her luxury room, with its four-poster bed, goose feather pillows, and roaring fire, brings her no comfort. She hates sleeping alone. If she could, she'd make a visit to the coterie to engage the services of one or two playmates, but High Council members are prohibited from doing so.

Making use of the coterie is a luxury afforded only to junior members of the coven in preparation for their ascent to the High Council. It gives young Mistresses an opportunity to explore relationships with a variety of potential companions, learning how to exert their authority and gaining sexual confidence along the way. Not that Coralie ever had any trouble with that. From the very outset, she knew she loved sex and wanted as much of it as possible, her insatiable appetite quickly gaining her a reputation for being hot cunted.

But such loose behavior is not considered appropriate for someone on the High Council. Now, she's expected to choose a bond and commence the very serious business of procreation. Fucking for fun isn't part of the agenda, which is already proving to be problematic, since her libido is stuck on full throttle.

To make matters worse, her room is across the hall from Mistress Isabelle's. The simple thought that Pet is so near, but tucked up in bed with another Mistress, probably screwing her senseless, is driving Coralie to the brink of insanity.

In desperate need of relief, she retrieves a sleek glass dildo from the bedside table and sets to work pleasuring herself. Lying on her back, as if ready to be mounted, she swirls the head of the dildo around her drenched slit.

"Oh, Pet," she murmurs, plunging the hard phallus deep into her sex. "I wish you were mine." She draws it out to the tip and drives it all the way back in, moaning as the tapered head bumps her cervix. "I want you to fuck me."

With increasing intensity, she works the glass cock inside herself, ramming it harder and faster until she screams through her orgasm, calling out Pet's name.

When her paroxysm passes, she pulls the slathered-up toy from her depths and tosses it onto the carpeted floor, sighing discontentedly. While moderately satisfying for a few fleeting minutes, it's a poor substitute for intimate contact. Something must be done.

Frustrated, she flings back the duvet and clambers out of bed, pulling a silk robe on over her negligee before padding quietly out of her bedroom, startled to find Pet sitting on the floor in the hall outside Isabelle's room.

The bashful brunette, caught off-guard by Coralie's sudden emergence, chews on her bottom lip, peering up at Coralie with raised eyebrows, her knees tucked up to her chin, looking every bit like a mischievous puppy.

Wondering why, Coralie takes but a step, her foot splatting in a puddle of warm fluid. Upon investigation, she's surprised to see a splooge of thick white milt squishing between her toes. And there's not just the puddle on the floor. Apparently firing without aim, Pet's emission is dripping down Coralie's door, the wall, and soaking the flowers in a nearby vase.

"Goodness!" Coralie lifts her foot, wiping it off on the hallway rug. "You really come in bucket loads, don't you? You messy little thing." She winks, showing Pet that she's not in the least bit upset. In fact, she feels strangely proud.

Knowing that Pet can't touch herself without explicit permission from her Mistress, she concludes that this rather sticky accident was the product of another uncontrolled eruption, only this time, Pet had the forethought to pull her priapus out of her pants before it was too late.

"I take it you heard me enjoying myself." Coralie sidesteps the rest of Pet's spillage and crouches beside her. "It wasn't my intention to tease you. I assumed you'd be engaged in some nocturnal activities of your own."

Pet scrunches up her nose and snorts, expressing revulsion at the thought of being intimate with her Mistress.

Curious for her to expound on that, Coralie presses the topic. "Are you not attracted to Mistress Isabelle?"

Afraid that she's been too free with her thoughts and feelings already today, Pet shies away, declining to answer.

Undeterred, Coralie tries a different angle. "What're you doing out here all alone, Pet? Are you not permitted to sleep with your Mistress?"

This, Pet answers by pointing upwards to a large skylight window in the ceiling. Up there, in perfect view, is the moon. It's not quite full, which means there's no chance of any copulation resulting in conception tonight.

"Ah." Coralie understands perfectly. "You're of no use to her, so you've been cast aside. How frightfully boring for you." An idea sparks, her eyes twinkling wickedly. "Would you like to come somewhere with me instead?"

Pet shrinks back, her brows knitted, pained to have to reject Coralie's invitation.

"Are you forbidden from moving?" Coralie guesses.

Pet nods.

"Very well." Coralie smiles broadly. "Then I shall bring the fun to you." She gets to her feet, ruffling a hand through Pet's hair. "I'll be right back."

She disappears down the hall and into darkness, but sure enough—and much to Pet's very pleasant surprise— she does indeed return several minutes later, wearing a grin and bearing a plate of food: cheese, bread, and grapes, all stolen from the kitchen.

"Food for your tummy." She sets the plate on the floor. "And food for your eyes." She straightens up, tugging the waist tie of her robe undone and opening it to unveil a short white silk negligee, the front laced from navel to bust, cinching her breasts into the corset-like garment.

As the robe slides off her shoulders, something in one of the pockets hits the carpet with a thud, but Pet's focus is elsewhere. Coralie still isn't wearing any knickers. Her sex is plainly visible, and—despite her recent release—Pet feels a certain part of her anatomy swelling at the sight.

"Peek-a-boo!" Coralie flips up the hem of the negligee, giving the lonely young companion a quick flash before lowering herself to the floor. "May I feed you?" She snuggles close, breaks off a piece of the cheese, and offers it to Pet's mouth, fully expecting to be rebuffed.

And she is. Pet closes her eyes, letting the cheese bump against her clamped lips, whining to let Coralie know how much she wants to accept, but that she's unable to take even one bite for fear of being unfaithful to her Mistress. They've already pushed too many boundaries.

Sympathetic to Pet's moral quandary, Coralie withdraws her hand. "I don't mean to make you uncomfortable. If you feel that it's improper for me to be so intimate with you, you may help yourself." She gives the plate a push, nudging it closer to her. "Please. You need to eat, love."

Pet's too hungry to argue. She takes a piece of cheese from the plate and brings it to her mouth, nibbling on the corner of it like a tiny mouse.

"Good, Pet." Coralie fingers Pet's long bangs out of her eyes. "I don't want you to go without. You must be absolutely ravenous."

For a few minutes, she lets Pet eat in silence, watching her devour the bread and cheese in hurried but dainty bites, wishing she could feed her the grapes. One by one. Slowly. Sensually. She tries to keep her thoughts away from sex, but every now and again, Pet's gaze wanders to her cleavage, lingering there for several seconds before shyness causes her to turn away.

"Do you like the way I look?" Coralie hooks her fingers around the neckline of her negligee and tugs the silk down a few inches, showing off more of her breasts. "There's no harm in looking." She pushes her palms up under her breasts, thrusting them together and outward, emphasizing the deep valley between them. "Do you want to see more?" She unties the bow at the bust of her negligee, loosening the lace, her breasts bulging forward.

Pet averts her eyes and fidgets awkwardly, crooking one knee to conceal her groin. As she does, she squeezes her eyes shut and holds her breath, trying to quell her arousal. It doesn't work, but she doesn't let out the breath that's trapped in her lungs until she feels Coralie's warm hand on her knee, coaxing her to be more open.

"Oh, darling. Please don't hide." Coralie fixes her eyes to the prominent bulge in Pet's crotch. "You're so beautiful." She holds her hand out, hovering inches away from Pet's lap, feeling the heat radiating from her erection. "If you were mine, I wouldn't let you spend the night anywhere but in my bed." She smirks, lolling against the wall. "Of course, I'd expect you to tend to me at all hours, putting your delightful assets to good use." She loops her arm through Pet's. "Do you think you'd like that?" She gives the timid companion a squeeze.

Pet would love to answer, but all she can think about is how one of Coralie's weighty breasts is smooshed against her arm. She remains silent, trying for all the world *not* to think about tending to Coralie's sexual needs, but Coralie isn't about to let her off the hook.

"Would you enjoy making love to me?" the seductive Mistress coos, caressing her would-be companion's chest.

In response, Pet groans softly. Leaning her head back, she savors the sensation of Coralie's hand making repetitive passes over her ribcage, rubbing just below her breasts.

"My sweet Pet." Coralie rests her head on Pet's shoulder. "You're driving me crazy."

At that, Pet breaks into a toothy smile and gestures to her turgid priapus, a small wet spot appearing at the tip.

Coralie chuckles. "I suppose I'm having a bit of an effect on you, too, huh?" She sighs wistfully, transfixed on Pet's anatomy. "Does Mistress Isabelle allow you to relieve your tension in any way?"

Pet shakes her head.

"Have you *ever* touched yourself?"

More forlorn shaking, a tear cascading down Pet's face, splashing onto Coralie's nose.

Saddened that Pet's sobbing, Coralie brushes the tear away, pressing her hand to Pet's cheek. "If I could release you from your bond to Mistress Isabelle, would you like that? Would it make you happy?"

Pet nods feverishly, nuzzling Coralie's palm.

"Then so it must be." Coralie kisses her teary cheek. "I will find a way." She brings her mouth close to Pet's ear. "I want you to be mine."

CHAPTER FOUR

DINNER IS A SEDATE AFFAIR. WHILE DISCUSSION AMONG many of the Mistresses inevitably revolves around fertility and conception, Coralie remains quiet. As the only unbonded Mistress at the table, she has nothing much to add on the subject, and all the talk of pregnancy makes her irritated and envious. Still, she manages to flash Pet a few forced smiles, silently assuring her that their exchange last night has not been forgotten.

Unfortunately, Pet is little comforted by those assurances. Impotent in her bond to Mistress Isabelle, she sees no possible way in which Coralie can procure her, and if she breaks her vow of fidelity, she'll be stripped of her collar and expelled from the coven.

Despondent, her thoughts heavy and her plate empty for the second night in a row, she curls up on her cushion beside her Mistress, watching beneath the table as Coralie taps the toe of one black stiletto on the floor in an impatient fashion, as if waiting for a train that's late to arrive.

She hopes for a replay of last night's flirtation, but nothing happens. This evening, Coralie is wearing a short, tight black dress, showing off her long, toned legs. She looks ravishing, and Pet would love nothing more than to crawl under the table and plant kisses on her cute feet. Her ankles. Her shins. Her thighs. Her cunt.

Willing an erection not to rise, Pet closes her eyes, trying not to think about sucking Coralie's fingers clean in the washroom. She'd never tasted anything as sweet. Coralie's sex was like liquid sugar on her tongue.

In comparison, she almost retches every time a drunken Mistress Isabelle drags her into bed, demanding oral pleasure. Not that it happens often. Isabelle's waning sex drive only seems to surface on moon nights, or when she feels like asserting herself as the dominant partner. There's no love shared between them. There never was.

Eavesdropping on tableside chitchat, Pet's ears prick when the conversation turns to the topic of Coralie choosing a companion. Not wanting Coralie to think her disinterested, she sits upright, making her presence known.

"I heard you had a rather uneventful presentation yesterday." The Mistress to Coralie's left pokes for details. "Is Diana preparing another selection for you this evening? You must make your choice by the end of the weekend."

"Another mundane parade won't be necessary," Coralie replies, meeting Pet's eyes across the table. "I know what I want."

"Is that right?" Isabelle finishes another glass of wine and glares at her, having caught the glance between them.

Not waiting for a response, she calls over one of the serving staff and demands a bottle of her special wine, the High Council's traditional elderberry wine being too weak for her taste. Angered that Coralie would dare to so brazenly make eyes at her companion, a fresh glass of booze isn't in her hand fifteen seconds before she downs it. A few seconds after that, she flops forward, her face smacking into her dinner plate.

The room falls silent.

Assuming she's passed out drunk, no-one does anything.

A full minute passes.

Alarmed, Pet doesn't know where to look. First, she stares at her unmoving Mistress, waiting for her breathing to resume. When that doesn't happen, she turns to Coralie.

In that moment, the Mistress beside Coralie lets out a gasp, watching in horror as the glow in Pet's eyes fades, signaling the expiration of her bond. At a loss for words, the Mistress points a finger at the now petrified companion, drawing everyone's attention to the ocular change.

It can only mean one thing.

Mistress Isabelle is dead.

Letting a small smile break free, Coralie sets down her knife and fork, dabs at her crimson lips with her napkin, and gets up. Her high heels clacking on the hardwood floor, she rounds the table, her pace slow and certain. When she reaches Pet, she unclips her from the chain attached to her collar, the other end of which is still clamped in Isabelle's dead fist.

"Come, my Pet." Coralie takes Pet by the hand, pulls her to her feet, and leads her around the table without saying another word.

As they approach her place at the table, Pet breaks away and darts in front of her, pulling the chair out for her, eager to win her appreciation.

"Thank you, Pet." Coralie pauses to kiss Pet's cheek before sitting down.

That simple act of thanks makes Pet blush uncontrollably. Settling happily into the appropriate spot on the cushion beside her elegant new Mistress, she takes advantage of the closeness now afforded to them and snatches up Coralie's foot. Unable to help herself, she brings her lips first to the shoe, then the ankle, gradually working her way up Coralie's leg, her hand following in the path of her mouth.

No longer required to keep her ministrations below the knee, her kisses keep going till she reaches the hem of Coralie's dress, whereupon she feels the tickle of Coralie's fingers on the nape of her neck.

Encouraged by that, she nudges Coralie's dress up with her nose, baring the top of her stockings and coming painfully close to exposing her to the room. There, she lays kisses on the soft, pale skin of Coralie's inner thigh, the pair becoming so wrapped up in one another that neither of them notices when two of the serving staff heave Isabelle's corpse out of her chair and unceremoniously cart her off for disposal.

Purring, Pet continues to nuzzle her face in Coralie's lap, nipping, biting, and kissing, hungering for her peachy skin and what lies above. At first, Coralie doesn't say a word, her arousal evidenced by her labored breathing, her lust-filled eyes, and the way she drags her fingernails through Pet's hair, but then ...

"Stop," she whispers softly, fisting Pet's mane, breaking her lips away. "You excite me too much," she explains privately, bending to Pet's level, pressing her mouth to Pet's ear. "You'll make me come."

At the head of the table, Mistress Diana clears her throat, diverting Coralie's focus from her new companion and securing the attention of the group.

"I take it by that rather shameless display of appetence that you intend to adopt Pet?"

"I do." Coralie strokes Pet's hair. "She's perfect."

Suitably calmed, Pet rests her chin on Coralie's lap, smiling up at her savior.

"Then I must ask you to tether her." Diana resumes her meal. "All companions must be tethered."

"Why?" Coralie refuses to comply. "I don't need a chain to keep Pet near me."

"If you wish to claim her for your own, you must exert your authority."

"And I must do that by restraining her?" Coralie peers down at Pet. "You know who your new Mistress is, don't you, Pet? You know who you belong to."

"She doesn't belong to you yet," another Mistress reminds her from across the table. "Not until you're bonded."

"That won't take long." Coralie fusses over Pet, straightening her hair and rubbing her back. "We're meant to be together. I feel certain of it."

"Lucky for you that Mistress Isabelle popped off, then."

"Quite." Coralie smiles sweetly. "And lucky for Pet, too, since Isabelle handled her appallingly. I wouldn't treat a dog the way she treated Pet."

"It's not for you to criticize others for the way they discipline their companions."

"It wasn't discipline, it was abuse," Coralie contends. "I will not ever use violence to assert my dominance. I don't want Pet to fear me, I want her to love me."

At that, Pet picks up her head, hardly able to believe those words just came from Coralie's lips. Love is a word seldom uttered at the High Council table. Companions serve a purpose, like a kettle or a teapot, and their humanity—their need for tenderness and affection—is rarely recognized.

Ignoring the rumbles of laughter circulating around the room at her expense, Coralie stands by her statement.

"I will earn that love, and honor it." She picks some food off her own plate and hand feeds it to Pet. "Hungry?"

Pet accepts the food without hesitation, sucking Coralie's finger into her mouth at the same time, no need for reservation anymore.

"Oh, you're such a darling." Coralie pulls Pet so close that she's practically draped over her lap. "I'm going to take such good care of you."

Post-dinner, the Mistresses of the High Council retire to the drawing room for an evening of champagne and bragging. Most use this as an opportunity to show off how well trained their companions are, but Coralie has little interest in competing.

She's sprawled on a chaise, her back propped on cushions, and while many other companions are set to work pleasing their Mistresses—whether by rubbing their feet, or performing sexual favors—Pet is curled up alongside her, half on top of her, one arm flung around her waist. She's sound asleep, her face pressed to Coralie's abdomen, murmuring every now and again as Coralie massages her scalp.

"You're coddling her," one of the other Mistresses warns Coralie.

Lying topless on another chaise, her breasts flattened against the velvet upholstery, Mistress Sirena—a curvaceous blonde approaching forty—has her own companion straddling her back, rubbing her shoulders.

Also topless, the companion's heavy breasts sway and bounce as she rocks her body back and forth, and Coralie is momentarily hypnotized.

"Pet deserves to be coddled." She snaps herself out of it, returning her full attention to her new mate. "She didn't get much sleep last night."

That piques Sirena's interest. "Last night?"

"Mistress Isabelle put her out in the hall," Coralie explains, leaving out the details. "She was sitting there all night, outside my room. Alone."

"Perhaps she was being punished."

"Or perhaps Isabelle was just a raging bitch." Coralie slams the door on that topic, leaving no room for discussion.

"Hmm. Well, whatever the case, Pet's absolutely besotted with you already. However did you win her over so quickly?" Sirena's tone carries an edge of suspicion.

"It wasn't magic." Coralie feels Pet's priapus twitch against her leg. "I haven't done anything but show her affection and kindness."

"Affection?" Sirena raises an eyebrow. "You know you can't make proper use of her until you're officially bonded. You should be trying to divine her true name right now instead of cavorting with her in front of everyone."

46

"We may not be able to have sex, or touch each other intimately, but that does not preclude affection." Coralie shifts her leg so that she can feel the full length of Pet's augmentation brushing up against it. "I will know her true name before the weekend's out."

Sirena snorts, disbelieving. "No-one's ever secured a natural bond so fast. It can take weeks or months to win the heart of a new companion."

"That may be, but I do not intend to be parted from her. I won't wait until the next gathering before I claim her, you can mark my words."

Sirena takes Coralie's confidence with a pinch of salt. Divining a companion's true name—the name she was given at birth; a name not uttered since her initiation into the coven—is no easy task, and neither party has any control over when it occurs. It's a subconscious reflex: an involuntary, psychogenic response signaling the companion's readiness to surrender themselves completely into the care of another. Only then will her name be known, and only if the Mistress is attuned to it. Unless, of course, you cheat.

The frustration of being unable to secure a bond gathering after gathering has driven many a good witch to resort to magic, and Sirena has her doubts that Coralie is capable of such patience. They've known each other for several years, and spent many a pleasurable time together in the coterie before Sirena's ascension to the High Council.

"Don't kid yourself. You want sex, and you want it now." She laughs. "I can loan you Brat, if you'd like. She'll fuck you three ways from Tuesday if I tell her to."

"I know." Coralie smirks at the red-headed companion sat astride Sirena's back. "We shared her in the coterie before she was yours. Remember?"

"You hogged her," Sirena grumbles. "You don't know how to share."

"As I recall"—Coralie challenges her version of events—"you loved to watch."

Sirena blushes."Do you want to play tonight? It's been a while since you and I have enjoyed each other's company, and Brat's hard as a rock already."

"I can see that." Coralie eyes the enormous bulge in Brat's crotch, her core tingling with the memory of being lanced by that thick pole. Brat's not particularly long, but her girth ...

"Do you want her to take it out?" Sirena watches the lust build in Coralie's face, her chest flushed with excitement.

It's not uncommon for Mistresses to share companions at these gatherings. Sometimes it's a straight swap for the evening, sometimes it's a foursome, and sometimes even the junior Mistresses are invited along to play. In fact, it's become standard practice among the High Council for the older Mistresses to watch their companions fuck the younger women, and Coralie was always high up on the list of invitees.

Her lack of inhibitions coupled with her enthusiasm for being gawked at made her an ideal candidate. As an added bonus, it quickly became apparent that there was very little she wouldn't do in the pursuit of pleasure.

But that was the past, and Coralie turns away from the view in front of her, removing temptation from her field of vision. "No, I don't want her to take it out," she answers at last, a trace of regret in her voice. "I want to wait for Pet."

Sirena giggles, amused by Coralie's rather uncharacteristic devotion and the outrageous notion of voluntarily going without sex. "Suit yourself."

"I always do." Coralie winks. "But it's getting late. We should be going to bed."

"We?" Sirena doesn't try to hide her surprise. "You're taking her to bed? What for?"

"More affection." Coralie tickles Pet's nose with her fingertip. "Wakey-wakey, darling."

Pet stirs, yawns, and stretches, writhing on Coralie like a cat. While her arms are lifted up over her head, Coralie swoops in and pulls her upward, manipulating her ninety-five pound frame with ease.

"Are you ready to call it a night?" She cradles Pet in her arm, smiling down at her.

Feeling playful, she tickles Pet's ribs, making her giggle and squeal, her limbs flailing and jerking, hearty laughter erupting.

All eyes fix on them, and as Pet becomes conscious of a change in the atmosphere of the room, she hushes herself, the disapproving glares of the other Mistresses causing her to retreat into the safety of Coralie's embrace.

"Ignore them," Coralie whispers in her ear. "They're just jealous." She slips her arms around Pet's tiny waist, lifting her off the chaise and planting her on her feet. "Come now." She leads Pet to the door. "Our bed awaits."

CHAPTER FIVE

AT CORALIE'S BEDROOM DOOR, PET COMES TO A DEAD STOP, digging in her heels as Coralie tries to drag her over the threshold.

"I want you with me, silly." Coralie chuckles, coaxing her forward, assuming her reluctance is due to some deeply ingrained low expectations.

But that's not it at all. Pet looks around at the remnants of last night's excitement. Cleaners have washed the floor and Coralie's bedroom door, but missed the sticky sheen on the flowers in the vase. Not knowing of any better way to explain herself, she plucks the head off a milt-coated rose and hands it to Coralie.

Eyeing the crusty petals, Coralie does her best to translate.

"Are you worried that you'll become too aroused?" She tucks the strong-smelling flower into her hair. "Or you think I won't be able to keep my hands off you?" She pulls Pet into the room and kicks the door closed. "I know the rules, love. I know them inside out and back to front, and they're very explicit." She steers Pet over to the bed, a fire already roaring in the hearth. "There's nothing whatsoever to dictate that we cannot undress for one another, or embrace. I can kiss you anywhere but your lips and ... well, any of the other obvious places. I can touch myself, you can watch, and we can attain shared relief—as you already know. We must use our imaginations, Pet. That's all."

Coralie takes a step back, allowing Pet's eyes to roam her body.

"Would you like to undress me?" she asks, lifting her hair up and out of the way.

Her hands shaking, Pet wipes her clammy palms off on her pants and moves behind Coralie, fumbling with the zipper on her dress. After several stops and starts, she manages to peel it all the way down to the small of Coralie's back, baring her snowy skin.

No bra.

No panties.

Pet's anatomy reacts predictably and her jeans tighten. Taking her time, she walks her fingers over Coralie's perfect skin, feeling the dimples at the bottom of her spine, following the curve of her back upwards to the nape of her neck.

Completing her circuit around Coralie she stands but a few inches away and slips the dress off her shoulders, lowering it to reveal two full, firm breasts. Glued to them, she's paralyzed, leaving Coralie to take over the removing of her own dress, wriggling it over her hips and letting it drop to the floor around her feet.

Indeed, Pet's so entranced by Coralie's full nudity that she temporarily forgets to be embarrassed about her arousal, her hefty priapus threatening to break free from her pants. Of course, when Coralie unintentionally snaps Pet out of her reverie by licking her lips and emitting a faint whimper of yearning, Pet covers her groin with her hands.

"There's no need to be shy." Coralie pries her paws away. "From what I've seen so far, you look exceedingly well-endowed."

It's true. Given Pet's small stature, her augmentation appears disproportionately huge.

"I'll bet that's why Mistress Isabelle chose you," Coralie says without thinking, Pet's arousal noticeably wilting at the first mention of her former bond.

"You know why I chose you?" She brushes Pet's bangs away from her forehead, trying to restore her excitement. "Your beautiful eyes." She holds Pet's gaze. "I can't wait until they burn for me as they once burned for her."

Just then, a gust of cool wind howls down the chimney, making Coralie shiver, reminding her of her nudity, goose bumps pricking her flesh.

"Would you fetch me a negligee?" She directs Pet to an antique armoire in the corner of the room. "Any one will do."

Pet opens the heavy oak door, coming face to face with more silk and lace undergarments than she's ever seen. Not knowing where to begin, she glances over her shoulder, hoping for guidance, but Coralie offers her none.

"You pick," she insists. "You'll be the one enjoying it, after all."

Her heart thrumming, Pet flicks through Coralie's wide assortment of nightclothes, bypassing any that fall below the knee and ultimately selecting a pink babydoll nightdress. Decadently translucent, the sheer, mesh-like material is accented with lace frills around the hem, and boasts a deep V-shaped neckline with narrow straps. Looking from Coralie's full bosom to the tiny scrap of fabric in her hands, Pet has trouble envisioning how it could ever contain her.

Coralie giggles. "If you're wondering how it manages to cover everything up, the answer is: it doesn't." She holds her hand out to receive it, and slips it over her head with a flourish.

Her breasts stretch out the bust, the narrow straps just wide enough to conceal her nipples and areolae, leaving the rest of her bosom exposed.

"Your turn," she declares then, grinning as she sits down on the edge of the bed facing Pet. "Will you take your clothes off now?"

Again struggling to control her trembling fingers, Pet undoes the first few buttons of her shirt, then catches sight of a purple, shoe-shaped bruise on her breast bone and stops. Ashamed of the marks on her body, she holds the shirt closed, fearful that Coralie will find her unappealing.

Glimpsing the perceived imperfection that Pet's so anxiously trying to keep hidden, Coralie takes action.

"You needn't be self-conscious." She eases Pet's hands away from the buttons and completes the work herself, pulling the shirt open. "I can make the hurt go away." She bends, pressing kisses all the way down Pet's sternum, gradually sinking to her knees.

As the first time, Pet closes her eyes, relishing the warm tingling of Coralie's magic.

It's over too soon.

"See?" Coralie smiles up at her. "Flawless." She runs her hand up between Pet's perky breasts, careful not to stray, then snakes her fingertip back down. "So beautiful," she murmurs softly, counting Pet's ribs, feeling her taut stomach, finally coming to a stop at the waistband of her pants. "Now take these off."

Blushing with a fury, but unable to deny the request, Pet unbuckles her belt, tugs down her zipper, and breathes an audible sigh of relief when her engorged priapus springs free.

"Oh, gods!" Coralie gawps at it, her cunt pulsing involuntarily. "You're magnificent!" Still on her knees, she leans forward for a closer examination.

Pet's blush intensifies. Not only is Coralie's face mere inches away from her throbbing erection, but she's a Mistress, and Mistresses don't kneel for anybody. Ever.

Though she tries to prevent it, a drop of milky anticipation oozes from the swollen head of her eager appendage, clinging there like dew on a petal. Worsening her condition, she watches with horror as Coralie opens her mouth and extends her tongue, ever so carefully touching the tip to the droplet, never letting skin touch skin.

"Mmm." She draws it into her mouth, her passions inflamed by the thought of the life it can create. "So potent."

Much to Pet's relief, she then gets back on her feet and clambers into bed, putting some distance between them. The respite is only brief, however, as she pats the mattress, inviting Pet to join her. Naked, of course.

Enticed as much by the big comfy bed as she is by Coralie's exquisite body, Pet sheds the rest of her clothes, wills her anatomy to behave, and prepares to flop into the sheets ... but then she spots a small bottle of liquid on the bedside table.

It's prussic acid.

Cyanide.

At that moment, a revelation hits and she feels foolishly naïve. First, there was the thunk she'd heard when Coralie's robe hit the hallway floor following her late night trip to the kitchens. Then, there was Mistress Isabelle's sudden death at the dinner table.

It was the wine.

Poisoned wine.

"Never look a gift horse in the mouth." Coralie winks, seeing the cogs whir in Pet's mind.

She's on her knees again, her arms outstretched, waiting for Pet to crawl forward on the bed and meet her in the middle.

"Someday, I plan to sit at the head of the High Council," she announces, placing her hands on Pet's waist, pulling her tight. "And I shall have you by my side, always and forever."

Pet reciprocates the hug, wrapping her arms around Coralie for the first time, relishing the contact until her priapus disgraces itself by slipping under Coralie's negligee and finding its way to her unprotected sex, nestling between her labia.

Coralie groans.

Pet gasps and recoils.

"Don't panic." Coralie peers down between them, the head of Pet's disobedient piercer now smeared with her juices. "It was an accident. I doubt they'd strip your collar and expel us from the coven for an unintentional slippage." She pecks Pet on the nose and lies down. "Now get under the covers before you explode!"

Bashful, and not at all sure how to keep her arousal under control, Pet gets into bed and tucks herself up with her back to Coralie. This situation is alien to her in a number of ways, not least of all because she's never known what it's like to have someone want to be close to her purely for her company, rather than to be used for breeding.

She and Mistress Isabelle didn't spend a single night together until after their bonding—which itself was the result of magic, with not an ounce of true feeling behind it—and even then, she was often booted out of bed when her Mistress was done with her. She's never before felt tenderness without agenda, or affection for affection's sake, and she tenses when Coralie starts tracing patterns on her bare back.

"Did Mistress Isabelle whip you?" Coralie asks, running a fingertip over one of many angry red lashes, this one extending from the small of Pet's back to her right shoulder blade.

Pet bobs her head twice for yes.

"Did you like it?" Coralie doesn't want to presume.

She's been with enough playmates to know that, for some, a little bit of pain and punishment adds to the flavor of sex, but it's by no means a pre-requisite of the collar. Unlike many of the other Mistresses, she doesn't view the infliction of pain as an expression of dominance. It's an aphrodisiac for some, but clearly not for Pet. The bed jiggles as she answers in the resoundingly negative and curls herself into a ball.

"Then it'll never happen again," Coralie assures her, laying kisses all over her back, healing the broken skin.

By the time she's done, the whole of Pet's back is tingling and warm, and Pet relaxes again, the tension in her muscles dissipating.

"There." Coralie sits up, happy with the results of her ministrations. "All better."

Unable to vocalize her thanks, Pet rolls onto her back and flashes Coralie a meek smile, keeping the covers pulled up to her chin, still overly concerned about her nudity.

"Look at you." Coralie sweeps hair out of Pet's eyes. "I think we need to trim your bangs. Or perhaps let them grow out." She tucks the tousled chunks of hair behind Pet's ear. "Whichever you'd prefer."

Bursting with happiness and gratitude for Coralie's good nature—such a relief from her former Mistress—Pet captures Coralie's hand and lavishes kisses on her palm. Her personal preference has never been taken into account for anything.

"If only I could kiss that mouth." Coralie sighs longingly, letting Pet kiss each of her fingers in turn before sucking gingerly on her thumb.

"I can't wait to hear your voice." Coralie keeps talking, as much to make Pet feel at ease as to distract her mind from the wetness between her thighs. "I already love your laugh, your giggle, and the little whimper you make when you come."

Pet's cheeks burn, but she resists the urge to hide.

"Did Mistress Isabelle let you speak much?" Coralie wonders, a companion's words reserved only for her bonded Mistress.

Instantly, all trace of a smile vanishes from Pet's face, sadness returning.

"Ever?" Coralie probes deeper.

Pet shakes her head.

"Well, I shall want to hear you talk." Coralie turns onto her back, going on to tell Pet how she likes to be vocal in bed, enjoys being given compliments—just like any woman—and how she wants Pet to know that her thoughts and feelings are valid. Unbeknownst to her, as she lazes there, the duvet drifts down below her bust.

Pet, her erection still raging, stares at the outline of Coralie's breasts behind the tight-fitting pink lace, her stiff nipples jutting out behind the gossamer fabric. After a few minutes of this, she rolls over and stares at the canopy above them, the duvet gripped tightly in her hands, her brow puckered with concentration.

Coralie stops mid-sentence. "What's wrong?" She shuffles closer to her mate. "Does it not please you to be in bed with me?"

Pet whines, wanting desperately to communicate the nature of her problem. In lieu of being able to use words, she lifts the covers an inch, gesturing to what lurks beneath.

Intent on breaking her of such chronic shyness, Coralie grabs a handful of the duvet and tugs it all the way down, revealing her achingly stiff erection lying on her stomach, leaking copiously into her belly button, a string of tiny white pearls gliding down the shaft.

"Oh!" Coralie beams, excited by the prospect of giving Pet another orgasm. "You really are the most perfect creature I've ever seen. Do you need to come, darling?"

Pet whines again, nodding vigorously.

"Then why don't you stroke it for me?" Coralie tickles her fingers along Pet's midriff. "Please."

Pet adopts a questioning look.

"Do it." Coralie cuddles up to her. "As much as I want to, I can't do it for you, and Mistress Isabelle is dead." She cradles Pet's neck in the crook of her arm. "There's nothing preventing you from enjoying yourself in this way. Not anymore."

Self-conscious, but willing to give it her best shot, Pet gathers up the thick webs of mucilaginous fluid clinging to the tip of her priapus and lubricates the shaft, tentatively wrapping her fist around it. She starts with one quick pull, testing it out, but soon falters. Before she gives up altogether, Coralie pounces on the opportunity to bolster her confidence.

"Like this." She closes her hand around Pet's, showing her how to move. "Does that feel good?" She pumps their hands up and down at a rapid pace, squeezing the crown at intervals, causing Pet's turgid augmentation to ooze a constant stream of pearly excitement.

Throughout, she whispers in Pet's ear, telling her—in deliciously graphic detail—all that they'll be able to do with one another once they're bonded, her erotic promises ending with a softly spoken command.

"Come for me, Pet."

Right on cue, Pet emits a muted squeak, her hips flexing involuntarily as a torrent of hot milt spurts from her priapus and puddles on her belly.

CHAPTER SIX

CORALIE AND PET WAKE IN EACH OTHER'S ARMS, CLEAN sheets and clean bodies. They're naked, breast to breast, Pet's small body curled into Coralie's secure embrace.

"Good morning, Pet." Coralie smiles down at her.

Pet returns the smile, but jerks away when she realizes she's woken with a stiffening and that it's pressed between Coralie's legs. Terrified by her unintentional recklessness, she leaps out of bed, grimacing apologetically.

"Don't worry, my love." Coralie stretches and yawns. "I'm not complaining. It was a nice way to wake up." She arches her back, displaying her breasts. "In fact, there's only one way it could've been better." She throws the duvet off her nude body. "Will you give me pleasure?"

Both of Pet's eyebrows go up, having not a clue what that might entail.

"My arousal might not be quite as obvious as yours, but I'm no less a slave to it." Coralie spreads her legs. "Lying next to you excites me like you wouldn't believe." She grabs her own breasts, squeezing them and teasing her nipples. "Pet, will you tend to me?"

Pet's priapus noticeably swells, but she stays put, guilt washing over her. Last night, Coralie had seen to her comfort. When it was over, they'd showered and changed the bed sheets, then she'd fallen asleep in Coralie's arms. She hadn't thought to return the favor—didn't know how she could—and Coralie hadn't asked ... hadn't given any instruction.

Sensing that Pet needs a gentle push, Coralie rephrases herself, wording her request in such a way that Pet can't possibly deny her. "Darling, I want you to make me come."

Crawling back onto the bed, Pet looks up and down Coralie's body, wishing she could touch. Exasperated by her helplessness, she reaches for Coralie's hand, places it upon the seat of her lust, and manipulates her digits, pushing two fingers between her plump labia and hoping that will suffice. But it doesn't.

"No." Coralie withdraws, shaking her head when she realizes what Pet intends for them to do."I don't want to touch myself this time." She trails her hands along her inner thighs. "I want you to kiss me." She scrapes her fingernails across her skin. "Right here, like you did at dinner. But this time, I won't tell you to stop."

Caving to her own desire as much as to Coralie's will, Pet repositions. She gets as close as she dares to Coralie's sex—which is close enough that her hot breath tickles her Mistress's weeping flesh, making her squirm—and blows directly on her clit.

"Mmm, careful." Coralie cups a hand over her core, hiding it from view. "Be so careful."

Doing precisely as she's told, Pet lays kisses all over her thighs.

Kissing.

Stroking.

Biting.

"Oh, gods, yes!" Coralie throws her head back. "Bite me harder."

Growling, Pet scrapes her teeth over Coralie's skin, marking her with passion.

"My Pet ..." Coralie begins to shake. "I'm so close."

Pet clamps her hand over Coralie's—the one protecting her treasure—and presses lightly, pushing Coralie's palm against her clit until she cries out, her entire body racked with spasms.

As the tremors ebb away, Pet raises up and cocks her head, wondering if Coralie enjoyed it. Which she did.

Breathless, Coralie beckons for Pet to lie on top of her. "That was perfect." She hooks a finger through the ring on Pet's collar, pulling her close. "So perfect."

On her hands and knees, keeping her body raised above Coralie's, Pet edges forward. As she does, Coralie spies her erection between them.

"We know what to do with that now, don't we?"

To make sure she doesn't accidentally poke Coralie in a forbidden place, Pet lowers herself down, pinning her priapus between their bellies. When she leans in for a nose rub, it squishes between them, causing the most delightful friction, and an idea blossoms. She rocks her hips forward, testing the sensation, then looks to Coralie for permission to continue.

"I don't see why not." Coralie glides her hands down Pet's bare back. "If it feels good, let it feel good." She grips Pet's firm rump and directs her thrusts, encouraging her to settle into a gentle rhythm.

It's almost like sex.

Almost.

Relaxing into it, Pet curls her arm under Coralie's neck, bringing them closer. Her weight supported on her elbow, she runs her free hand over Coralie's waist and hip, breaking eye contact only to peek down at her Mistress's unrestrained breasts, watching them jiggle with the motion of their bodies.

In short order, her priapus starts to leak. Coralie's soft belly becomes slippery and wet, their movements becoming sloppy and frantic until Coralie can't take it anymore. She whispers the magic words—"Come for me, Pet"—and not a second later, a splash of warmth coats her chest.

Following another shower, Coralie and Pet arrive late for breakfast, both entering the drawing room wearing smiles of sexual satisfaction—much to the consternation of Mistress Diana. The aging coven leader knows full well that if any rules had been broken, so too would the spell cast upon Pet when she was first initiated into the coterie. She finds their intimacy perplexing.

"Sorry we missed breakfast." Coralie smoothes out some creases in her knee-length skirt and straightens the cuffs of her white blouse. "We were a little preoccupied."

"What did you two do last night?" Mistress Sirena smirks at them from a couch by the fireplace. "You're both glowing like hundred watt bulbs."

Grinning, Coralie plants herself on the other end of the couch, gesturing for Pet to sit at her feet. "We enjoyed each other in any and every way that we could." She rubs Pet's shoulders, encouraging her to snuggle close. "And then again this morning."

Sirena's eyes widen. "But you didn't … ?"

"Of course not." Coralie flexes her ankle as Pet bends to deliver a flurry of kisses.

This time, Pet slips off Coralie's shoe and fondles her stockinged foot, rubbing her toes, her arch, her heel, and laying kisses on her at intervals. When she stumbles upon a ticklish spot, Coralie murmurs, her toes curling, her lower lip caught between her teeth.

"You've got it so good." Sirena sighs wistfully, watching Pet go to work. "I practically have to beg Brat to rub my feet. Do you have any idea how undignified that is? And I swear she hates every bloody minute of it."

"Well, I can't help you with your companion problems"—Coralie whimpers when Pet sucks a toe into her mouth—"but I can confirm that I'm a *very* lucky woman." She thinks especially of Pet's beautiful anatomy.

"You're *about* to be," Sirena corrects her. "If you can intuit her true name."

Pet's ministrations falter.

"All in good time." Coralie keeps her tone neutral, wholly unconcerned.

Sirena laughs. "I think you forget how well I know you. If you don't get laid soon, you'll self-destruct. Are you sure you don't want to borrow Brat for a quickie?"

Pet's face falls, her hands dropping from Coralie's foot.

"Quite sure." Coralie cups Pet's head in her hands, letting her know, beyond any doubt, that it won't happen. "I'm waiting for Pet."

"That's cute." Sirena rolls her eyes. "But you might want to be careful. The way you're flaunting her is starting to rile up some of the other Mistresses."

"Are you saying I might have some competition for Pet's affection?" Coralie feigns shock. "You think it possible that her head could be turned by another?"

As a demonstration of her commitment, Pet rests her chin in Coralie's lap, purring.

"Perhaps I might want her for myself," Sirena teases. "Would you consider a trade?"

"Don't bother," a Mistress on the other side of the room cuts in on their conversation. "I've heard Pet's unable to perform."

"Is that so?" Coralie curls a lock of Pet's hair around her finger, eyeballing the envious Mistress with a sour glare. "You think she's impotent?"

"She spent over six months with Mistress Isabelle, and there was no pregnancy to show for it."

"That drunken old wench was probably barren." Coralie isn't at all ruffled by the rumor. "Pet was wasted on her."

Growing self-conscious, the direction of the conversation venturing into unflattering territory, Pet turns her head in Coralie's lap, keeping her face averted from the rest of the room, thereby concealing her unease, anxiety, and fear of inadequacy from everyone but Coralie.

"Pet." Coralie pats her lap, inviting her onto the couch.

Pet tilts her head, questioning the invitation. It's customary for companions to sit on the floor at their Mistresses feet. Then again, it's also customary for a companion to be tethered, and Pet hasn't seen her chain since Coralie adopted her.

Coralie pats her lap again, repeating the offer. "Come on up." She holds her arms open. "I want a cuddle."

For once in her life, Pet's small stature proves beneficial. While most other companions wouldn't fit comfortably in their Mistresses laps—not that they'd ever receive such an invitation to begin with—Pet is small enough and light enough to curl into Coralie's arms, her head tucked on Coralie's shoulder.

"That's better." Coralie wraps one arm around Pet's waist, stroking her legs with the other. "I like having you close." She kisses the top of Pet's head. "You make me so happy."

Brimming over with desire and adoration, Pet pushes her face against Coralie's neck, her hand slipping from Coralie's shoulder to rest above her heart.

In that moment, something passes between them. Coralie gasps and clutches Pet's hand, her heartbeat rising from a sedate sixty to almost a hundred. Caressing Pet's head, holding her tight, she moves those long, scruffy bangs aside, tucking them behind her ear, then she leans in, whispering softly so that only Pet can hear ...

"Mieka."

Pet lifts up her head, locking eyes with Coralie, her irises shimmering and gleaming, brightness returning to them as a new bond forms.

"Oh, my darling. My Pet." Coralie's eyes drop to Pet's mouth, wanting nothing more than to taste those baby pink lips. "Kiss me."

Pet does just that. Their mouths meet, no reservation and no timidity. Hungry for intimacy, Coralie captures Pet's lips with her own and flicks her tongue in between, her advance met with equal enthusiasm, their tongues battling for entry into each other's mouths.

In the midst of it all, Coralie drops her hand to Pet's crotch, finding the stirrings of an erection and quickly massaging it to full rigidity. Then, she breaks the kiss.

"I think we should go back to bed, don't you?" She palms Pet's expanding appendage. "Otherwise, they might have to call someone out to reupholster this sofa." She lifts Pet up and deposits her on her feet, turning her in the direction of the door.

Lightheaded, Pet sways from side to side, all the blood that should be in her brain now diverted below her waist. Coralie rises to steady her, but they don't get to take a step.

"What in the gods names do you think you're doing?!" Diana swoops over to them, alerted to their lustful behavior by the same woman who called Pet impotent, but when she sees Pet's burning, iridescent eyes, she backs down.

"She cheated!" The envious Mistress accuses Coralie without missing a beat.

"I did no such thing!" Coralie snarls back. "We were right here the whole time. How could I cheat in plain view of everyone?"

Diana questions Sirena on that. "What were they doing?"

Sirena shrugs. "Cuddling."

"Cuddling?" Diana pulls a face.

"Yes, you know." Coralie tugs Pet close to her, squeezing her erection to keep it firm. "It's that thing you do when you really like someone and you want to show them how much they mean to you. Now, if you'll excuse us both"—she grips Pet's proud augmentation, showing Diana the prominent bulge in her pants—"we have a rather urgent matter to attend to."

CHAPTER SEVEN

CORALIE PULLS PET INTO THE BEDROOM, BOMBARDING HER with kisses. Staggering backwards toward the bed, she keeps her lips clamped over Pet's, gripping Pet's shirt in her hands. When she backs up against the bedpost, she slides her hands over Pet's chest, fumbling for her belt.

"I want you to fuck me," she growls, tearing the belt away.

Reengaging Pet's mouth, she sucks hungrily on her tongue, ready to feel a pair of groping paws delving up her skirt. Instead, Pet's kiss lacks passion. She's reciprocating, but it's weak, her hands resting limply on Coralie's hips.

She's overwhelmed.

Intimidated.

Coralie can see the conflict in her eyes: desire strangled by fear.

"I'm sorry." She forces herself to drop into a lower gear. "Am I going too fast?" She takes a deep breath, licking the taste of Pet's kisses off her lips. "I need to remind myself how young you are. You were poached by Mistress Isabelle on the day you were initiated into the coterie. You've only ever been with one woman, whereas I've ... had experience."

Pet doesn't mean to, but she winces, her reaction betraying some prior knowledge.

"Did you hear anything about me before we met?" Coralie feels a faint twinge of shame. "Did you know my name?"

Pet nods, unable to look Coralie in the eye.

"Did you hear stories about me?" Coralie assumes.

Pet shakes her head, touching a fingertip to the corner of her eye.

"You saw me?" Coralie translates. "Where? Talk to me, Pet. You can now, and I want you to." She slumps against the carved oak bedpost. "Where did you see me?"

Pet clears her throat, preparing to speak for the first time in ... she can't remember.

"I ..." Her voice cracks and she coughs, her mouth suddenly dry. "You were invited up to the drawing room one night." She hesitates. "To be with one of the other companions."

"Ah." The twinge of shame blooms into full-on regret. "You saw me fuck."

"It was Brat." Pet keeps her head angled down. "You looked like you were enjoying yourself, and I don't want to disappoint you, that's all."

"I can't imagine that's possible." Coralie smiles reassuringly. "But let's slow down." She taps under Pet's chin, requesting that she look up. "We'll go at your pace, not mine."

Pet opens her mouth to say something, but Coralie puts a finger to her lips, silencing her.

"Hush now, Pet." She takes a step back, dropping her hands to her sides. "Explore me, and take your time. There are no limits now, and there's nothing whatsoever to be afraid of."

Given free rein, Pet smothers her anxiety and places her hands on Coralie's body, beginning at her waist and moving over her ribcage, up to the underside of her breasts. They're more than a handful each—for her petite mitts at least—and she groans as she lifts them into her palms, feeling the weight of them.

She needs more.

Letting them go for the moment, she reaches for Coralie's shirt buttons, waiting to receive a nod of approval before she forges on.

"Go ahead," Coralie urges her. "Undress me."

Her hands shaking, it takes Pet forever and a year to get halfway down, by which time she loses patience with herself and wrenches the shirt open, sending tiny plastic buttons scattering across the room.

Pet fears a rebuke, but far from being angered, Coralie moans her appreciation for the momentary loss of decorum.

"Keep going." She shrugs the shirt off her shoulders, slinging it to the floor.

Today, she's wearing a bra, and Pet struggles with the front clasp.

"Relax." Coralie stays her hands, afraid that she's about to destroy the tailor-made lingerie. "I need some of my clothes to make it through this unscathed."

After a brief pause to collect herself, Pet pops the clip on her first retry. Coralie's breasts spill free, and she engulfs them with her hands, feeling two stiff nipples graze her palms.

Watching her push them together then release them, letting them bounce, Coralie giggles.

"Mine are bigger than Mistress Isabelle's, huh? More fun to play with."

Pet nods, her eyes never leaving Coralie's chest. They're bigger, firmer, and altogether more delicious, and she rubs her thumbs over both erect nipples, teasing them harder.

"Use your mouth, Pet." Coralie wraps her hand around the back of Pet's neck "Bite."

That's not a command Pet needs to hear twice. Still kneading one breast, she sucks the other swollen nipple into her mouth and clamps her teeth around it, giving it a gentle tug.

Her legs weak, Coralie clutches the bedpost for support. "Bed." She forces Pet to stop suckling on her. "Let me get into bed before I fall down, love."

Remembering that Coralie has other assets yet to be bared, Pet curls a finger around the waistband of her skirt and follows it around till she finds a zipper. Expecting to discard the garment and find nothing beneath, she's surprised to discover that Coralie's wearing undies.

Coralie laughs, shimmying them down to her ankles. "I can be modest sometimes." She kicks off her shoes and props her foot up on the bed, about to roll one of her stockings down.

Pet stops her. Enjoying the way Coralie looks in the hosiery, she runs her fingers up the fine silk, relishing this moment.

"You like?" Coralie parts her legs a few inches. "If you keep going, you might find something you'll like even more."

Pet pulls her hand away.

"Boo." Coralie pouts. "Are you teasing me, Pet?" She yanks the duvet off the bed and lies down. "I thought that was my job."

Standing at the foot of the four-poster, Pet removes her clothes in a flash and tosses them to the floor on top of Coralie's. With as much composure as she can muster, she then creeps up the bed on all fours and positions herself above her new lover, swiftly resuming her sucking, pinching, biting, and kneading.

After fifteen minutes, her sex flooded and throbbing, Coralie plucks Pet's hand off one of her breasts and moves it down to her core, placing it directly on her mound. "My cunt is weeping for your touch."

Hints don't come less subtle than that.

Pet tickles her fingers through Coralie's curls, seeking out the hidden pink below. There, she finds Coralie hot and wet, her labia engorged with lust, and she pushes inside. Her middle digit slips into Coralie's slit and she swirls it around, feeling the soft, pulpy flesh of her insides.

"More," Coralie demands.

Pet adds another finger.

"More," Coralie insists again.

Though it feels impossibly tight, Pet eases in a third finger, groping her until ...

She stops, her expression pained.

"What is it?" Coralie props herself up on her elbows, her head spinning with endorphins, her body on the brink of an orgasm. "You nearly had me."

Keeping her fingers embedded, Pet rocks back on her heels and shows Coralie the state of her swollen anatomy. It's leaking all over the bed sheets, ready to burst.

"Oh, my love ..." Coralie brushes her finger against the tip, wetting it with Pet's eagerness. "You know what you ought to do with that now, don't you?"

Pet has no idea.

Yearning for it, Coralie wraps her legs around Pet's waist. "Fuck me, Pet." She writhes on the sheets. "I need it now."

She closes her eyes and waits, but nothing happens. When she opens her eyes again, she finds Pet steeling herself for the task of penetration. The young companion is grimacing like she's about to drive a stake through someone's heart, her tongue pinched between her teeth in deep concentration, all hint of pleasure absent from her fraught expression.

"Whoa." Coralie places her hands on Pet's chest, preventing her from driving forward. "Why are you making that face? Talk to me again, Pet."

Pet hangs her head. "I ... I've never ..."

"You've never had sex?"

"Not like this." Fearing inadequacy, Pet softens. "I've used my mouth and fingers, but never my ... thing-um-bob."

"You're a virgin," Coralie whispers, amazed.

"Does that disappoint you?" Pet expects the worst.

"Oh, gods, no!" Coralie's eyes gleam. "I'm surprised, that's all. I mean, I know you're young—so deliciously young—and I'd considered that you might not be as experienced as some of the other companions, but I never expected ..." She fawns over Pet's body. "How could that beastly Mistress Isabelle have had you to herself every night and not absolutely ravaged you whenever she had the chance?"

"She did." Pet sighs. "At least, she tried to on moon nights, but I couldn't ... and my poking thing wouldn't ..." She makes an 'up' motion with her hand, indicating her inability to generate an erection for her former Mistress. "She thought me defective."

"Well"—Coralie grins, reaching between them to grip Pet's sticky pole in her hand, coaxing it to fatten again— "we know differently now, don't we?"

"You seem to inspire the opposite problem in me." Pet gawks at Coralie's nudity. "I haven't been able to keep it down since we met. You gave me my first stiffening."

"I'm glad it was me." Coralie pushes her onto her back. "But that must mean Mistress Isabelle never tended to your physical needs."

"Tended to them how?" Pet frowns.

"Like this." Coralie straddles her, fondling and kissing her small but perfectly-formed breasts, pausing only to look up and gauge her reaction. "Or how about this ..." She kisses her way down Pet's belly.

Wriggling lower, she drops a kiss on the underside of Pet's priapus.

And another.

Another.

She works her way from the root all the way up the full length of Pet's eight-inch shaft. When she gets to the crown, she dips back down, running the tip of her tongue along the path of her kisses. Reaching the crown again, she swirls her tongue around the head, causing a bead of pre-fuck to appear.

"Is that for me?" Coralie laps it up, wrapping her lips completely around the tip.

"No, no, no!" Pet panics, her hands flailing around Coralie's head, not daring to pull her away, but so desperately wanting her to stop.

"What is it?" Coralie releases Pet's appendage with a sloppy pop. "You don't like it?"

"No, it's ... you shouldn't have to ..." Pet's brain stumbles over all the words she wants to say, in the end reducing the problem to its simplest form. "You're my Mistress."

"And?" Coralie sits astride Pet's crotch. "Do you not think it proper for a Mistress to please her companion in that way?" She pins Pet's augmentation in the valley of her sex. "Do you think it demeans me? Do you think it undermines my authority if the focus is on your pleasure instead of my own?" She leans forward, whispering in Pet's ear. "That's bullshit."

Still, Pet looks conflicted.

"My darling, Mistress Isabelle didn't treat you well." Coralie mashes her breasts to Pet's chest. "She didn't understand what it means to be a Mistress, but I do." She grinds herself on Pet's erection. "I want to take care of you in *all* ways. I want to make you happy as much as I want you to make me happy. It's all about *mutual* pleasure, Pet."

"But—"

"Sshhh." Coralie snatches up her hand, kissing the tip of her thumb. "Think about how good this would feel elsewhere on your body." She sinks her mouth around the digit, simulating fellatio, first taking an inch, then more.

Gradually, she increases speed and intensity until she's sucking on it furiously. Pet starts bucking up into her, desperate for stimulation, but Coralie lifts her hips, raising her crotch and withdrawing contact altogether, waiting for ...

"Please," Pet begs hoarsely, frustrated that she's humping nothing but air.

Coralie pulls her mouth off Pet's thumb. "Please what?" She wants her to say it.

"Please use your mouth."

"Be more specific. You want me to use my mouth where? Here?" She pecks Pet's cheek.

Pet giggles. "No."

"Then where? Maybe here?" She bites and kisses Pet's neck.

"Na-uh." Pet squirms beneath her.

"How about here?" Coralie engulfs one of Pet's nipples in her mouth.

"Mmm, nope."

"So tell me." Coralie peers up at her lover. "Where?"

"Please suck my thing." Pet's voice is so quiet it's barely audible.

"Say again?" Coralie cups her ear, pretending she didn't hear. "I don't think I heard you."

Being overly diffident, Pet sweeps her bangs down in front of her face, shielding herself, never imagining in her wildest thoughts that she would ever be asked to say these words in the presence of her Mistress. "Please suck my thing-um!"

"Is that what you want, Pet?" Coralie circles her finger around the smooth head of Pet's priapus. "You want me to lick you here?"

Pet whines, writhing beneath her, incapable of words.

Deciding she's been tormented enough, Coralie rewards Pet with her mouth. She swallows as much as she can, sucking on it till Pet's ready to come before pulling back and letting the imminent threat pass. This, she repeats five times, and after a while, Pet catches on: Coralie's not going to let her come until she begs for it. Coralie is in control.

"Please," Pet implores her the next time she eases off. "Let me come."

Her eyes closed, she waits for the return of Coralie's mouth, but instead, her vestal augmentation is enveloped in heat and forced into something much tighter. Yowling, she looks down, finding Coralie impaled on her.

"You're not a virgin anymore, Pet." Coralie raises up and slides back down, lowering herself slowly over the shaft so that Pet can watch it disappear within her. "How does it feel?"

Pet's mouth opens, but no sound comes out. Having once witnessed Coralie with Brat in the drawing room—an energetic fuck with Coralie on all fours, being rammed into from behind—this isn't at all what she imagined sex would be like. Coralie's movements are languid and unhurried, calm and tender.

"Do you like making love with me, Pet?" Coralie coos, working herself on the thick rod buried inside her.

Yes, Pet thinks—that's the difference! This is lovemaking, not fucking. It's a glorious thought, and one that threatens to tip her over the edge. Almost immediately, she feels a distinctive pressure in her abdomen and her face creases with tension.

Understanding her problem, Coralie slows to a near stop. "It's all right. This is your first time, and I've been teasing you dreadfully. Just let yourself go." She picks up the pace again. "Whenever you want to."

Other companions would be severely chastised for succumbing to their crisis before ensuring their Mistress has reached at least one pinnacle, but Coralie isn't so selfish.

"It's coming already," Pet whimpers, lifting her head to watch Coralie ride her, whining and mewling at the sight of her priapus being swallowed up by Coralie's sex. "It's coming, it's coming, it's coming ..."

"That's it, Pet." Coralie squeezes her muscles around Pet's erection. "Come inside me."

Pet cries out, jerking her hips up as Coralie bears down. Driven instinctively to deliver her gift deep inside Coralie's womb—moon night or not—she hilts herself, grabbing the older woman's hips and crushing their bodies together.

Her unexpected forcefulness catches Coralie off-guard, causing a small paroxysm to ripple through her. She tries to count Pet's ejaculatory contractions, but loses track at ten.

"You're so virile!"

She's ecstatic, but Pet looks ashamed.

"I'm sorry I didn't last."

"Don't be sorry, Pet. Things are going to be very different for you from now on." Coralie remains skewered. "I'll be patient, and I'll train you well."

"I want to please you."

"And you will." Coralie feels Pet move inside her. "You're starting to get hard again already—ah, delicious youth!" She lifts herself off Pet's hot lance and rolls onto her back. "I want you on top." She positions herself for sex. "Don't be too afraid, and don't hold back if you want to come again. You probably won't last long the first few times, but I shan't be angry. Endurance will come with practice, and let me assure you, I shall be giving you plenty of practice." She winks.

Pet tries to say something else, but Coralie silences her with a kiss.

"Hush now, Pet." She pulls her new companion onto her. "Just make love to me."

Part Two

Fulfillment

CHAPTER EIGHT

Six weeks later ...

CORALIE'S BLOOD RED FINGERNAILS SCRAPE AGAINST HER Egyptian cotton sheets, clawing and gripping at the fabric. Loose curls of her long raven mane spill over her white pillowcase, tousled from sleep and the tug-and-pull of night-long sex, and she comes again, grinding her core into Pet's face.

Having woken from fevered dreams, her heart pounding and her body pulsing with lust, she'd been pleased to find her bedmate similarly aroused, and promptly took advantage of a willing and highly skilled tongue. Twice.

Her second climax subsiding, she giggles, feeling her lover's tongue snake up her body, and she lifts the covers, peering beneath to welcome Pet up for air.

Naked but for her collar, Pet emerges from the southern realms of the king-sized bed in Coralie's decadently decorated bedroom, licking her bare pink lips and savoring every last drop of Coralie's precious honey. Her odd-colored eyes burn with lust for her Mistress, her bangs now trimmed so as not to conceal them.

"Good morning, my love." Coralie cups Pet's cheeks and draws her into a kiss, emitting a faint 'oomph' when she feels the tip of her companion's rigid priapus slip between her labia, nudging her opening.

"Ooh," she murmurs, wriggling her hips to embed the phallus deeper, though only by an inch. "Do you want to fuck me, Pet?"

Pet dips her head and groans with need, but waits for permission to push forward. She'd woken up with a stiffening, tiny beads of anticipation already forming, but she must wait a little longer for her pleasure.

Taking hold of Pet's hips, Coralie jerks her pelvis up and down, rubbing the head of Pet's oozing hardness along her slit.

"My darling," she coos, feeling a copious amount of pre-ejaculatory fluid smearing onto her already slick flesh. "Is all that excitement for me?"

She continues to tease, denying Pet entry while stimulating her to the point of causing small shudders to ripple through her body. Then she clasps her hands to Pet's cheeks, forcing the trembling brunette to make eye contact.

"I want you inside me, Pet."

Wasting no second, Pet drives forward and pierces Coralie, hilting herself on the first thrust and moaning in unison with her Mistress. Quickly working up a rhythm, she pumps her weeping anatomy into the very deepest part of Coralie's sex, eliciting a series of vehement affirmations punctuated with various wails and whines.

Thirty minutes in and three orgasms later, Coralie clutches Pet's rump, pulling her tighter. "So close again, my Pet." She digs in her nails. "So close!"

Pet, too, is on the cusp of her inevitable peak. Struggling to keep rhythm, she begins to shake, her breathing labored. Pressure is building at the base of her augmentation, and she clenches her muscles, determined to hold back her release.

It starts to hurt, but she grits her teeth and forges on. After another minute of vigorous fucking, her brow creases and she chews hard on her lower lip, drawing blood, her pained expression signaling her desperate need to come—something which she cannot do until Coralie permits it.

Sensing the strain in Pet's body, Coralie lifts her head, bringing her lips to Pet's ear. "Come for me, Pet," she whispers, both giving her consent and issuing an order.

Dutifully—and thankfully—Pet lets herself go. Growling and grunting, she quickens her pace, stabbing into Coralie with as much force as she can muster until she feels Coralie's muscles tighten around her and she achieves the pinnacle of her pleasure. As heat burns up her shaft, she buries herself deep inside Coralie, the swollen head pressed firmly against her Mistress's rubbery cervix, flooding her womb.

When it's over, she lowers herself on top of her Mistress, panting heavily.

"Is that better, Pet?" Coralie strokes her hair.

Pet nods and whimpers, too weak to move.

"Me, too, darling." Coralie kisses the side of her head. "You please me like no-one else ever has, and if I'm not very much mistaken ..." She grabs Pet's bum and rolls her hips, sliding herself up and down Pet's length. "You're not done pleasing me yet. You're still so hard." She pulls Pet into a kiss. "It must be because this evening will be the first night of the full moon."

Pet looks uncomfortable, her euphoria fading.

"I'm ready when you are." Coralie keeps humping her. "You know that."

She's hoping for another round of sex—with any luck, a prelude to a night of intense lovemaking fueled by a mutual yearning to conceive—but instead, she feels Pet's anatomy shrivel inside her. Disappointed, she releases her grip on Pet's rear and lets her pull out.

When their union is broken, she peers down, saddened to see that Pet's lost all trace of her erection. In fact, she's lost all trace of her priapus. In its place, a perfect vagina is nestled between her legs, her distinctly female sex ornamented with a triangle of bushy brown pubic hair.

"What am I doing wrong, Pet?" Coralie sits up, the shift causing Pet's seminal deposit to begin its downward descent. "Why does the thought of giving me a child kill your desire for me?"

Pet wriggles to the edge of the bed, staring dismally at her altered genitalia, knowing from experience that it could be hours before the thing returns to its augmented state.

"Talk to me, Pet." Coralie shuffles up behind her, rubbing her shoulders. "You know I'll never make you do anything you don't want to do, but I need you to tell me what's wrong."

"I know." Pet sighs. "You've been so patient."

"I understood why you didn't feel ready on the last moon." Coralie's shoulder rub turns into a full-on massage. "We'd only been together for a few days. We were still getting to know one another, you were shy, and I didn't want you to think I was merely using you for breeding."

Pet cringes. "I wish you wouldn't say things like that."

"Why?" Coralie's ministrations cease.

"Being with you is so confusing." Pet begins to sob, overwhelmed by Coralie's compassion. "The way you treat me goes against everything I was taught to expect from this life. You're *supposed* to use me for breeding. That's the whole point of me. It's my purpose."

"But, darling"—Coralie turns Pet to face her—"I don't want you to sire your first progeny just because it's expected of you. I don't want to conceive knowing that you have no emotional investment in my pregnancy. This should be something that we do *together*, because we both want to have a child."

"I *do* want to." Pet sniffles, tears streaking down her face. "I dream about it all the time. Awake or asleep, I can't get the thought out of my head."

"Then what's the problem?" Coralie's heart swells to bursting, Pet's confession very nearly bringing her to tears of her own. "What're you so afraid of?"

Pet's brow creases with an insecurity Coralie hasn't seen since their first night together.

"Just ... what if I can't?" she says slowly.

"Can't what?" Coralie strokes her back, coaxing her to open up.

"Fill my purpose." Pet pats her bangs down over her forehead, even though they're now far too short to hide behind. "If I can't give you what you need, then you won't want me anymore. You'll give me the boot and—"

Coralie tugs Pet's hands away, cupping her clammy cheeks. "What makes you think you won't be able to fill your purpose?"

"When I was with Mistress Isabelle, this always happened." Pet jabs a finger at her feminine parts. "So it's true what everyone says: I'm broken."

"It's all right, love." Coralie tries not to stare at the beautiful pink cleft hiding at the apex of her thighs. "It happens to all young companions at some time or another. It certainly doesn't mean you're defective. Learning to control the emergence of your secondary assets can take time."

"Control it?" Pet appears genuinely confused.

"Well, yes, of course." Coralie frowns. "Have you never been told? You can will your priapus away whenever you so wish. For a short time at least."

Pet digests that, her cheeks turning a fiery shade of red at the thought of all the indignities her unwilling appendage has caused her. "Mistress Isabelle didn't care for my innie bits. When I couldn't perform for her, she'd ..." At a loss for words, she holds out her index finger, hoping that the visual clue will suffice.

It doesn't.

Coralie looks thoroughly bewildered.

"It was the only way she could get me to come," Pet explains, growing more uncomfortable by the second. "It prevented me from losing the necessary parts, and the effect was pretty much instantaneous."

"I don't understand." Coralie shakes her head, unable to fathom it. "What did she do?"

"She'd stimulate me inside." Pet flops onto the bed, hiding herself in the crumpled bed sheets, muffling her words. "In my bum-be-doo."

"Oh ..." Coralie works that over in her mind, absently fondling one of Pet's tightly clenched buttocks. "Did you like it?"

Pet lifts her head up so that Coralie can see the scowl plastered on her face.

"Okay." Coralie holds up her hands, surrendering. "I was only asking."

"It's embarrassing." Pet plunges her head back into the sheets. "She made me ejaculate into a teacup, then she'd scoop it onto her fingers and—"

Coralie snorts, suppressing a laugh, resulting in another scowl.

"I'm sorry." She covers her mouth. "But a teacup? Really? My love, you could not possibly be contained in a teacup. You practically flood me every time we couple."

"It wasn't like that with her," Pet mumbles into the duvet.

Getting the distinct impression that this problem will not be so easily swept away—Pet's fears and insecurities well ingrained in her—Coralie cuddles up to her.

"Listen to me, darling. It wasn't your fault. Isabelle was an older woman, and it's no shock to me that she wasn't able to conceive with you. As far as I'm concerned, you've got no reason to believe that you won't be able to get me pregnant."

"But what if?" Pet clings to her pessimism.

"All right." Coralie shrugs. "What if? What do you think would become of you?"

"I'd be relegated to the coterie."

"Says who?"

"Mistress Isabelle." Pet rolls onto her back, peering sorrowfully up at Coralie. "Not that I cared much what happened to me then."

"But you do now?"

Pet's eyes fill with fresh tears. "I don't want to be with any other Mistress."

"Then we're perfectly suited," Coralie assures her, breaking into a smile. "I don't want to be with any other

84

companion." Her smile broadens. "Gods, you have no idea how relieved I am to hear you say these things."

"Why?"

"Because I was starting to think you hated the thought of siring my children. Now I know you're just sensitive. More so than the playmates I've been with. For them, sex isn't as meaningful. They're driven by their need for pleasure—the coterie instills that in them—and when they become companions, they don't think twice about cementing their bonds with their Mistresses by impregnating them. But you ..." Coralie dries Pet's cheeks. "You value our relationship above and beyond your biological imperative, and I like that. It means I'm more to you than just a fertile uterus waiting to be filled."

Pet giggles, amused and gladdened by the positive spin Coralie's able to put on her misplaced anxiety, and equally by the notion that it's possible for a Mistress to feel used by a companion. She'd never before considered that Mistresses might not be so impervious to bouts of low self-esteem, or that companions could be motivated enough by their own self-interest so as to reduce the act of procreation to little more than a strategic ploy intended to ensure loyalty.

But it makes sense. Once a companion sires a child and proves their potency, it's virtually impossible for them to lose their place. A Mistress can't cast aside her bond without good reason, and as soon as a companion shows that they're capable of fulfilling their purpose, the bond is secured indefinitely. For most, that's enough. Love is incidental, if it exists at all.

Still, despite Coralie's attempt to allay her concerns, Pet remains in turmoil.

"We're leaving for the next gathering tomorrow." She picks at a chip in her nail polish, having twice refused Coralie's attempts to remove the week-old color. "What will you tell them? This is our second moon already, and they'll be expecting ..."

"I know." Coralie slides off the bed, retrieves polish remover and cotton balls from the adjoining bathroom, and returns with a purpose of her own. "I'll tell them the truth." She douses one of the cotton balls in the strong-smelling acetone. "There's no shame in it."

"They'll laugh." Pet sits on her hands, eluding Coralie's efforts to snatch them up.

"So?" Coralie topples Pet over, straddling her belly and seizing one of her paws. "They laughed at me when I said I'd divine your true name during our first weekend together, and look how that turned out."

"Please don't." Pet's sorrow returns to her as the wet fluff ball touches her index finger.

"Why not? You've been fighting this for days."

"No-one's ever painted my nails before." Pet admires the cracked purple on her other hand. "I like that you did."

"And I will again." Coralie leans forward to rub noses with her. "I just can't have you looking like a ragamuffin tonight. You remember that we're having people over?"

"Girls." Pet nods. "Wannabes."

Coralie laughs. "I think they prefer the term neophytes."

"I don't care what they are." Pet pouts. "They'll never be half as wonderful as you."

"No?" Coralie starts work on a second nail.

"Not even a little bit. You're the best Mistress any companion could have."

"I'm glad you think so highly of me." Coralie temporarily abandons the cotton balls, pinning Pet's arms to the bed above her head and kissing her. "You know I'm the black sheep of the High Council."

"I don't care what color sheep you are." Pet moons up at her. "You're beautiful."

"So are you." Coralie trails one hand down Pet's body. "In all your forms." She tiptoes her fingers over Pet's mound, combing them through her pubic curls and working downward toward the slit. "I wish you'd let me show you."

"I'm not what you want. Not like this." Pet recoils, sweeping Coralie's wandering hand away and refusing to accept the intimacy, just as she'd done during the last moon. "Don't pretend."

"What makes you think I'm pretending?" Coralie juts out her lower lip.

"I don't have what you need." Pet wriggles away, tucking herself into a ball. "I can't please you when I'm this way." She shields her loins with the duvet, one hand covering her groin for added protection. "Not completely."

"Oh, yes you can." Coralie giggles. "And I can please you in a whole lot of new ways, if only you'd allow me to."

"That can't be true." Pet sniffles. "You like ... the other thing."

"I like penetration," Coralie clarifies, "and you can still give me that if you want to." She pulls a glass dildo out of a drawer in the bedside table and tosses it onto the bed. "But it's this I'm attracted to." She strokes Pet's face. "And this." She runs her hand over Pet's chest, waist, and stomach. "My darling, I'm gay. You're exactly what I want, no matter what you've got between your legs at any given moment."

"What about when you ... with your mouth? I thought you enjoyed that?"

"Are you talking about oral sex?" Coralie smirks devilishly. "To tell you the truth, the night we bonded was the first time I'd ever taken a priapus in my mouth. I never did that for any of the playmates I was with—I never had the inclination—but I wanted to do it for you." She presses a kiss on Pet's lips. "Trust me, it was about *you*, not your anatomy."

Offering up more kisses, she paints invisible patterns on Pet's skin, her fingers leaving a trail of heat in their wake. First, she makes circuits around Pet's breasts, arousing her nipples without ever pawing on them directly. Moving lower, she tickles Pet's ribs and makes her squirm. Finally, she splays her hand out over Pet's stomach, her electric touch causing goose bumps to prick her young lover's skin.

"Stop." Pet whimpers.

"Why?" Coralie sucks one of Pet's nipples into her mouth, directing her magic there. "Am I turning you on?"

Her hand makes the final trek to Pet's core, cupping her sex.

All seems to be going well, but then Pet panics. Desperate to prevent Coralie from investigating the core of her femininity, the petrified brunette flails and kicks her legs, accidentally striking her Mistress in the chest and knocking her backwards off the bed. As Coralie hits the floor with a yelp, Pet scrambles to her feet and flees to the bathroom, slamming the door behind her.

When the shock subsides, Coralie surveys the damage. Stunned but unharmed, she picks herself off the floor, covers her nudity with a silk robe, and knocks on the bathroom door.

Silence.

"Pet, come on." She knocks again. "I want to talk to you."

She tries the handle.

It's unlocked.

Going in, she finds Pet sitting in their large ceramic bathtub, her knees pulled up to her chin, crying so hard she's almost choking, her shoulders heaving.

"Let's sort this nonsense out, Pet." Coralie sits down by the side of the tub, resting her arms on the rim. "What happened back there?"

Pet says nothing. Struggling to find a way to express herself verbally, she turns over in the tub, maneuvering herself onto her hands and knees, presenting her bum to Coralie.

"What're you doing?" Coralie gives her a light spank.

"I hurt you," Pet wails. "You should punish me for it." She sniffles, tensing her body in preparation for pain, her forehead pressed against the cold porcelain.

"Oh, Pet." Coralie pats her baby soft rump. "I'm not going to chastise you. You shouldn't be punished for an accident."

She dives forward, biting one of Pet's butt cheeks, eliciting a muted squeak of surprise, then gives Pet a push, rolling her into a sitting position.

"It wasn't your fault." She strokes Pet's hair. "I wanted to try something new and it failed miserably. It's not the end of the world." She peers down at Pet's hitherto untouched sex, suppressing her yearning for it. "You're not ready." She averts her eyes. "I want you to be, but you're not. Perhaps we could try again another time, yes?"

"You really want me that way?" Pet mulls over the possibility.

"More than you can imagine," Coralie assures her, hoping she may yet warm to the idea. "I've been with many of the other Mistresses over the years, and plenty of women outside the coven. I love every inch of the female form." She pauses. "Will you consider it?"

Pet nods.

"Good." Coralie beams, taking her hand and pulling her out of the tub. "Now let's put this unfortunate business behind us and get ready to receive our guests."

CHAPTER NINE

CORALIE'S MULTI-MILLION POUND KENSINGTON HOUSE, like so much else about her, is far from modest. Dressed in textured wallpapers, with shades of red, purple, and gray throughout, it's bold and modern. Pet was afraid to touch the crystal door knobs for the first week, and it took her another six days before she'd sit on any of the furniture. Right now, Coralie's young dinner guests are having similar troubles.

The three teen girls come from very different backgrounds. One hails from a family farm in Wales, another from a pair of lawyers in Bristol, while the third—a gobby, pink-haired urchin—resides in Kent. All three, however, have one thing in common: they were born witches.

Nearing the age of eighteen, it's time for them to join a coven, but to do that, they must be referred by an existing member of the High Council. Tonight, that's Coralie. Their future rests in her hands, and so far, she's unimpressed. The shyest one didn't know which knives and forks to use for which course at the dinner table, the most apathetic one farted and blamed it on the cat, and the pink-haired one can't keep her lecherous eyes off Pet.

As they retire to the drawing room, Pet brings in a pitcher of lemonade for the girls and a glass of elderberry wine for Coralie, doing so without making eye contact with anyone. Perturbed by the pink-haired neophyte's quirky smiles and flirtatious glances, she turns to leave, but Coralie's sultry voice stops her by the door.

"Pet, don't go."

Nervous but obedient, Pet turns, drinking in Coralie's appearance: a plum-colored satin blouse, combined with a knee-length black pencil skirt and the black stockings and stilettos she always wears. Tonight, her long, curled hair is half-up, the front pulled back, keeping it out of her face, and her freshly painted fingernails are the same color as her lipstick. She looks reserved and sophisticated, which is a far cry from the unrestrained vixen she is in bed.

"Come." She pats her lap.

Trying to ignore the three strange pairs of eyes now following her every move, Pet pads to Coralie's side and sits at her feet, some of her discomfort abated simply by being so close to her doting Mistress.

In a way that's become routine for them, she strokes Coralie's crossed legs, silently worshipping her. Quite often, they'll sit by the fire at night, Coralie reading, Pet kissing and caressing. Invariably, Pet starts off on the floor, but always ends up in Coralie's lap, or lying beside her on the couch. Sometimes, Coralie will read aloud to her. This happens particularly when the book is of a steamy nature, thus ensuring that they tumble into bed pre-heated. But things are set to go a different way this evening.

As Pet runs a hand up Coralie's leg, the pink neophyte spots her painted nails, noting that both companion and Mistress are wearing the same shade.

"That's cute." She smirks, pointing. "You have matching color."

Coralie scoops up one of Pet's hands and kisses her fingers. "Pet picks what color she likes, and I paint them for her." More kisses. "Her toes, too."

"You do what she wants?" The neophyte laughs. "Shouldn't it be the other way around?"

"I take care of all Pet's needs, whatever that may entail," Coralie clarifies her position. "A companion should always be kept happy."

"I'm looking forward to having my own." The girl sips her lemonade, eyeing Pet like she's a thing meant to be devoured. "How do you keep her in line?"

"Keep her in line?" Coralie throws the question back at her. "You presume Pet to be disobedient?"

The girl half-shrugs. "I dunno. I guess I just wanna know how you assert yourself when you seem so good to her. How does she know who's boss?"

"Only people who lack control feel the constant need to assert it," Coralie educates her ignorant guest. "In any case, Pet was a rescue and I'd never hurt her."

"A rescue?" The belligerent teen pulls a face. "Like one of those sad-looking puppies at the animal shelter?"

Ignoring the attitude, Coralie answers with facts. "Pet belonged to another Mistress before me. I adopted her."

"You took someone else's seconds?" The girl wrinkles up her nose.

"Her first Mistress beat and abused her terribly." Coralie trails a finger along Pet's neck. "The wretched woman hurt my darling little Pet, and I couldn't let that continue."

Pet suppresses a whine, Coralie's magic touch making her skin tingle.

"I knew from the first moment I saw her that she was destined to be mine," Coralie goes on. "We couldn't keep our eyes off each other, could we, Pet? Our eyes, our hands." She slips her hand around Pet's neck, sending a surge of electricity through her young companion's body.

"What happened to her?" One of the quieter neophytes asks fearfully, mildly unnerved by Coralie's manner. "The other Mistress, I mean."

"She's dead." Coralie keeps her eyes on the mewling, purring creature in her lap. "Nobody will ever mistreat Pet again."

As the tingling sensation in Pet's body extends below her waist, causing her priapus to stiffen in a matter of seconds, Pet angles herself away from the couch, hiding her arousal from the three curious teens ... but not before one of them catches a glimpse of what she has to offer.

"Can I see it?" the pink-haired neophyte asks boldly, leaning in for a closer look.

Pet grabs a nearby cushion and holds it to her crotch, flashing Coralie a look of pure fright. She's known other Mistresses to be so proud of their companion's goods that they'll jump at the chance to show them off to anyone who asks, but she doesn't want to be put on display. Fortunately, Coralie is equally disinterested in turning her into a spectacle.

"I don't share," she responds calmly, dragging her fingers through Pet's mane. "Pet's body is for me, and me alone."

"Just a peek," the girl pleads.

Coralie rolls her eyes. "Fine." She winks at Pet, then turns to the ballsy neophyte. "But first, show me your cunt."

The girl's smile drops and she stares at Coralie, open-mouthed. "What?"

"You heard me."

The girl holds down her skirt, as if it might fly up of its own accord. "I don't want to."

"Then what makes you think Pet wants to show you her intimate bits and pieces?"

"I just thought ..."

"You thought her feelings didn't matter?" Coralie challenges her. "You thought I'd make her expose herself for giggles? You thought wrong." She invites Pet up into her lap. "Pet's feelings matter to me, as your future companion's should matter to you." She accepts Pet nuzzling her neck. "Companions aren't toys." She locks eyes with the pink-haired girl. "If you want a toy, might I suggest you get one that's battery operated. In the meantime"—she beams a fake smile—"would anyone like something else to drink?"

94

Coralie emerges from her en suite bathroom wearing her sexiest lingerie—a red and black satin corset with matching knickers and stockings—and is immediately disappointed, but not surprised, to find her bedroom conspicuously empty. Pet's nowhere to be seen. Donning a silk robe, she treks downstairs and locates her reluctant companion in the drawing room, clearing up empty lemonade glasses and cookie crumbs.

"Leave it. It's bedtime." She lingers by the door a moment, letting Pet get a good look at her, then walks away, knowing that her obedient companion will follow close behind.

Upon entering her bedroom, she discards her robe to the floor and stands at the foot of her bed, hands on hips, waiting. And waiting. Then Pet peeks around the corner, takes one look at her, and drops to all fours, crawling across the heated hardwood floor toward her Mistress.

Keeping her hands at bay until she's given permission to touch, she begins her kisses at Coralie's feet and works her way up. As she reaches the apex of Coralie's thighs, she's rewarded with the slight parting of legs, allowing her access to the pungent fruit hiding between, and she doesn't hesitate to take advantage.

Her first kiss lands on Coralie's mound, over her thick triangle of wiry hair, then she moves lower. She kisses the top of Coralie's cleft, finding her clit and sucking it into her mouth, the damp fabric of Coralie's knickers rich with the taste of her arousal. Lower still and she tongues Coralie through her underwear, making her tremble.

"Take them off." Coralie sways unsteadily, using Pet's shoulder for support.

Pet reaches up and fumbles for the waistband, but Coralie slaps her hands away.

"Use your teeth."

Complying willingly, Pet clamps her teeth around the hem and pulls the sodden undies down to Coralie's ankles with one swift tug, quickly returning her mouth to work.

In an effort to remain upright, Coralie grabs hold of the bedpost and lifts her foot onto an ottoman pushed against the end of the bed, anchoring herself as Pet dives into her crotch.

"Is my little Pet hungry tonight?"

Pet growls into her flesh, probing between her labia.

Coralie chuckles. "You know I can't finish standing up, don't you?" She fists Pet's mane and tears her away. "I need to lie down."

Dashing away from Pet's eager tongue, she drops onto the middle of the bed and awaits the resumption of Pet's oral stimulation. Instead, Pet scrambles onto the bed and unbuckles her jeans, preparing to release her revived priapus.

"Oh, gods, yes!" Coralie's eyes spark and she helps Pet pull the jeans off her hips, freeing her erection. "Pet, are you sure?"

Pet frowns, her head cocked.

"Have you forgotten?" Coralie massages Pet's seemingly eager anatomy, directing her attention to the large sash window beside the bed.

Outside, the white, round moon is in full view and Pet hangs her head, her enthusiasm softening in Coralie's hand, then vanishing altogether.

"Not again!" Coralie throws her head back, grabs a pillow, and holds it to her face, smothering a scream.

Humiliated, Pet slides off the bed and pulls up her jeans, ready to retreat to the guest bedroom, as she did on the last moon, but she doesn't get far.

"Wait." Coralie flings the pillow away and calls her back. "You're not excused."

Pet hovers by the door, keeping her back to Coralie, afraid of being reprimanded.

"There are other ways you can give me pleasure." Coralie's voice softens. "In fact, I have an idea." She delves inside the bedside table, fishing out the glass dildo. "Will you use this on me before you go?"

Pet pivots back to the bed, excited and terrified in equal measure. Coralie tosses the toy onto the mattress and lies in wait, her legs apart, her knees bent to the ceiling.

"Wet it first," she instructs.

Pet picks it up and wraps her hand around it, moving it several times through her fist, testing how it feels, learning the weight and the shape of it.

"It's okay, my darling." Coralie reads her trepidation. "Use it just as you would your own. It won't break, and you won't hurt me."

Apprehensive, but ready to do just about anything if it means making Coralie happy, Pet wets the toy with her saliva and nudges the tip to Coralie's pink. Using her thumb and forefinger, she spreads open the folds of delicate wet flesh, giving her an unobstructed view of Coralie's swollen opening as she pushes the phallus through.

Coralie groans, feeling the hard shaft filling her. "Deep and fast, Pet. Make it good."

Despite being somewhat distracted by her first bird's eye view of Coralie's tight sex being ravaged mid-fuck, Pet does her best, even managing to generate a wail when she accidentally discovers her Mistress's g-spot.

"Oh, that's it!" Coralie clutches Pet's wrist, making sure she targets the right area. "You have no idea how much I wish this was you."

Pet stops abruptly.

Realizing her mistake, Coralie offers a swift apology. "I shouldn't have said anything. I'm sorry." She encourages Pet to continue. "Go ahead and finish me with the toy."

Utterly disappointed—with herself and the whole evening—Pet's gusto for the task wanes. She halfheartedly wiggles the dildo, sliding it back and forth with ease, but Coralie's no longer making those wonderful noises, cheering her on.

Eventually, Coralie calls a halt to the torture. "This isn't working." She brushes Pet's hand away and removes the hot, slick glass shaft, banishing it to the bedside table. "Do you want to try something else instead? Perhaps something else we've never done together."

Pet looks blank.

"We can have penetrative sex," Coralie suggests. "But rather than putting your priapus in the usual place, you put it ... elsewhere. Somewhere there's no risk of conception, thus no reason to be afraid." She palms Pet's crotch, testing to see if the proposition results in any anatomical changes.

It doesn't, but under her ministrations, Pet begins to swoon. Taking a chance that she might now be receptive to stimulation of a different kind instead, Coralie slips a hand inside her open jeans.

"Talk to me, Pet." She eases her fingers between Pet's thighs. "Have you ever been touched like this before?"

Pet shakes her head, emitting a startled squeak as Coralie's finger grazes her clit.

"Do you like it?" Coralie circles that firm nub, then slips down to tickle Pet's labia, probing deeper to see if her ministrations are having any effect. "I can tell that you do." She dips her fingers in the moisture she finds there. "You're getting wet for me already."

"I feel so strange." Pet shivers, her toes curling. "I'm not sure what to do."

"You don't have to do anything." Coralie teases her weeping flesh. "Just let me take care of you the way you've taken care of me countless times." She pulls her hand back, sucking her damp fingers into her mouth. "Mmm, you're so yummy." She licks them clean. "I'll definitely be needing some more of that."

Without further ado, she divests Pet of her clothing, lies her down, and shuffles into position, kissing her way over Pet's mound. Salivating at the thought of driving her tongue into her young companion's needy flesh, she pulls Pet's folds apart with her thumbs, baring the flushed inner pink, and ...

"Oh, Pet!" she squeals gleefully.

"What?" Pet props herself up on her hands and looks down, expecting bad news. "You hate it? I knew you would."

"No, silly." Coralie slaps her thigh playfully. "My darling, you have a hymen!"

"So?" Pet looks perplexed. "Is that a good thing?"

"You're a virgin again!" Coralie claps her hands together. "It's exciting, no? I took your virginity once, and now I get to do it all over!" She dives back down, opening Pet up for another look. "This beautiful, maiden pussy ..." She flicks her tongue over Pet's clit. "All mine."

Her last words are muffled as she buries her mouth in Pet's sex, devouring her without hesitation or delicacy, alternating between attacking her clit and pushing inside her.

At the onset, Pet yowls, instinctively parting her legs wider and reaching for the back of Coralie's head. Every lash of her tongue feels like liquid fire, and Pet sizzles helplessly, utterly at her mercy. Brought to the brink of climax over and over again, but repeatedly denied release, she's reduced to a mewling mess of trembling limbs in no time at all. She knows this game well.

"Let me come," she pleads, unable to take another minute of such exquisite torture, her body in spasms, her breathing ragged. "I want to come in your mouth."

Say no more.

Coralie sucks hard on her clit, gliding a single digit through her opening to maximize the stimulation, and Pet's first girl orgasm crashes over her, the experience so overwhelming that she very nearly loses consciousness.

Leaving her there to recover, Coralie strips off her corset and retires to the bathroom to brush her teeth. When she's done, she hopes to crawl into bed and fall asleep with Pet in her arms, but she's destined to be disheartened. By the time she returns to the bedroom, Pet's gone.

Saddened that Pet's still shying away from her, she wraps herself in her robe, traipses down the hall, and enters the guest bedroom, finding pajama-clad Pet curled up in the bed.

"May I tuck you in?"

Pet nods happily and shuffles over, giving Coralie enough room to sit on the edge.

"You know we have an early start in the morning." Coralie peppers her cheeks with kisses. "Why don't you try to wake up before me, come to my room, and surprise me with your mouth? I'd like that."

As she leans forward for more kisses, her robe falls open, partially revealing one of her breasts, and Pet's eyes wander.

Coralie follows her wayward gaze. "You like what you see?" She shifts around on the bed, leaning against the headboard and stretching her legs out in front of her, flicking her robe over her knees. "Want to see more?" She tugs open her robe, completely exposing one of her breasts, and crooks her arm around Pet's shoulders, bringing her closer, coaxing her to take the firm nipple in her mouth.

Needing very little in the way of encouragement, Pet hugs Coralie's waist and starts suckling, surprised when, after a few short minutes, she tastes a few drops of hot milk on her tongue. Startled, she pulls back, another droplet clinging to Coralie's nipple.

"It's okay," Coralie urges her to resume. "It's part hormonal, part magic. I can only make it happen on moon nights, and I can make it stop if you don't like it."

Considering that for less than a second before arriving at a decision, Pet sticks out her tongue and laps up the single creamy drop before sucking the nipple back into her mouth, purring as she drinks.

Content with this intimacy, Coralie holds Pet to her chest, closing her eyes and relaxing, letting Pet take her fill. She notices that Pet's priapus returns to her and stiffens, tenting out her pajamas, but she doesn't draw attention to it. After a good twenty minutes, Pet falls asleep, her mouth still clamped around the now swollen nipple.

Smiling, Coralie eases her off and lies her down, kissing her forehead. "Sleep well," she whispers, turning the light off on her way back to her own room.

CHAPTER TEN

CORALIE AND PET SIT SIDE BY SIDE, NO SOUND BUT THE
rumbling engine of the limo and the crunching of pebbles
beneath wheels as the vehicle snakes its way along the
narrow roads to the desolate stone mansion where they'll
be spending the weekend.

Since getting into the car, Coralie's been waiting for
Pet to display some small modicum of sexual interest in
her, but so far, she's been let down. Having woken alone,
much to her chagrin, she'd dressed in one of her least
conservative skirt suits in the hope of making the long
journey more enjoyable by arousing Pet's interest, but
Pet's anxiety about the gathering is proving too all-
consuming to allow for the distraction.

After fifteen more agonizing minutes, Coralie finally
breaks the silence.

"Ugh, I can't stand this!" She slouches theatrically,
letting go of the tension she's been carrying in her body
all day. "We've been in this car for over three hours, and
you've yet to steal even a single glance at my legs." Trying
to lighten the mood, she smacks a kiss on the side of Pet's
head. "I'm not used to being so overlooked by you."

Pet stares at her hands, fussing with her nail polish,
knowing that none of the other companions will be
wearing any and that it's likely to make her a target for
mockery.

"I missed you last night." Coralie reaches for Pet's
hand, preventing her from picking at her nails. "I know

we haven't been together long, but already I loathe spending nights alone." She pulls Pet's hand into her lap. "Don't you feel that way?"

Pet manages a small nod.

"I missed you this morning as well." Coralie upturns Pet's hand and traces patterns on her palm. "I thought you were going to wake up early and surprise me."

For the first time since getting in the limo, Pet smiles, but it doesn't last long.

"Oh, do stop fretting." Coralie wraps her arm around Pet's shoulders. "I can handle the other Mistresses." Determined to brighten things up, she lets her gaze fall to a small lump in Pet's crotch. "I saw you get a stiffening last night while you were drinking from me." She palms Pet's limp priapus. "It was very erotic. It turned me on."

The lump grows and Coralie tickles her fingers over it, feeling the blood rush in.

"I love watching you grow." She shifts sideways, getting a better grip. "I love feeling you harden in my hand." She unfastens Pet's pants and tugs them down around her ankles. "Do you want to fuck me?"

Pet rather gets the impression that question's rhetorical. She can see the need in Coralie's eyes. It's more than lust, more than desire, and she recognizes it immediately: it's the same face she wore when she fucked Brat in front of all the other Mistresses.

"I'm sorry," Coralie apologizes in advance for her prurient behavior. "I need this." She pulls off her knickers and straddles Pet's lap. "I need *you*." She grabs Pet's priapus and sinks down on it, taking it all at once. "Moon times make me so damn horny."

Pet's not complaining, but having made a mess of anything even remotely resembling enjoyable penetration last night, and being too afraid to initiate a do-over this morning, she's leaking into Coralie within minutes, and Coralie's not going easy on her. But that's the plan.

"We need to be quick, okay?" Coralie works her vigorously. "I just want you to come." She grinds her pelvis in circles, experimenting with different sensations, ultimately finding the one that'll make Pet spill. "I want to feel it."

The closer Pet gets, the harder Coralie rides her, driving her toward completion. In the end, the sex lasts all of ten minutes, and concludes with Pet emptying inside Coralie seconds before the limo pulls up outside the mansion, their union leaving a puddle of milt on the leather upholstery.

Following a rushed attempt to make themselves appear presentable, Coralie and Pet descend upon the busy entrance hall holding hands, their closeness turning heads. Even the other companions—all unhappily chained to their Mistresses—make a point of scowling at Pet, openly resentful of how well she's treated by Coralie.

"Your stuff is gushing out of me." Coralie adjusts her skirt. "If I wasn't wearing knickers right now, I'd really be in trouble."

Again, the juxtaposition of Coralie's sophisticated demeanor with her rampant sexuality has Pet silently amused, but from there, the tone of the gathering tumbles downhill fast. First, Mistress Diana spots them from across the room and strides over, a glass of champagne in one hand, her companion's chain in the other.

"Still no tether?" She's quick to pick fault.

"Still don't need one," Coralie retorts, reserving Pet's tether for the rare occasions her young companion is in need of the added security it provides—which isn't often.

Though Pet's been trained to stand at least one pace behind her Mistress's shoulder at all times, Coralie flouts tradition and tugs her forward, looping their arms together. Whether she's doing so because she wants Pet by her side, or simply because she wants to irk her elders, the result is a whole lot of disdainful looks and much more attention than Pet would like.

Another Mistress—one Pet recognizes as the envious witch who accused Coralie of cheating at the last gathering—is quick to throw in her own snarky comments.

"How trim you look." She eyes Coralie's flat belly.

"How subtle you are." Coralie flashes her a saccharine smile.

"Well, why no pregnancy?" the Mistress keeps prodding. "This is your second moon."

"We're working on it." Coralie kisses Pet's head, taking the disapproving glares and the snide remarks in her stride. "And I think we need a little more practice, so if you can bear my absence, Pet and I are going to get settled in upstairs." She pulls Pet toward the staircase.

Inside their bedroom, she's pleased to discover a fire already lit and their suitcases deposited by the bed. It's warm, it's inviting, and she gets straight down to it.

"I think a nice hot bath is in order. How about you?" She strips off her knickers. "At the very least, I need a change of clothes. I'm drenched." She tosses the dripping panties into a nearby laundry hamper. "And things are probably getting uncomfortably sticky in your nether regions, too." She grabs a fistful of Pet's waistcoat and pulls her closer. "So how about it, Pet? Bath or shower?"

Pet separates from her and bounds into the en suite bathroom to draw a bath, finding a selection of oils and bubbles into the bathroom cabinet. Unable to pick just one, she pours a concoction into the water, resulting in a potent floral aroma and an over-abundance of bubbles that splurge out over the sides of the large, oval tub and onto the heated tile floor.

"Goodness!" Coralie appears in the doorway, sans jacket and cufflinks. "I can't leave you alone for two seconds, can I?"

She shuts off the water before it reaches the overflow, and sticks her hand in to check the temperature. As she bends over, Pet ogles her derrière, unaware that a mirror on the far wall is reflecting her interested eyes right back at Coralie.

"I hope you're going to do more than gawp." Coralie gives her bum a wiggle.

Holding that position, she waits for Pet to make a move on her, but Pet, put on the spot and taken by surprise, shoves her hands in her pockets and looks away.

"You don't always need to wait for express permission to touch me, Pet." Coralie spins on her heels and backs Pet up to the counter. "When we're alone, I'd like to think that you feel comfortable enough to flirt with me, hold me, and kiss me at will. Your advances will never be met with anything but warmth and reciprocation."

She grabs Pet's rump and lifts her up onto the counter, making her gasp.

"Of course, I have no problem taking the lead." She locks her lips over Pet's, giving her a tender, closed-mouth kiss. "But it's also nice to be shown that you want me as much I want you."

Pet directs Coralie's attention southward, the degree of her yearning made obvious by the physical reaction Coralie always provokes in her.

"I suppose that's true." Coralie giggles, unfastening Pet's pants and relieving the pressure for her. "You are in possession of a very reliable barometer of your affections."

Pet's crusty priapus flops out.

She raises an eyebrow at it. "You're definitely getting this bath with me." She smirks, unbuttoning Pet's waistcoat. "There's room enough for two."

Amidst kisses, and after some hasty undressing and the addition of a few extra bubbles, Coralie ties up Pet's hair, then her own, and sinks into the sudsy water.

"Come here." She grabs a sponge. "Let me wash you, you dirty little monkey."

Grinning from ear to ear, loving to be cherished by her Mistress, Pet steps into the water and plants her bum between Coralie's legs. Less than graceful, her sudden descent sends miniature waves crashing over the rim of the tub, bubbles slopping everywhere.

In the midst of the tsunami, Coralie scoots up behind her and squeezes warm water over her shoulders, scrubbing every inch of her back before slipping her hands under Pet's arms and soaping up her chest.

"Such a dirty little monkey," she repeats softly, kissing Pet just below her ear. "My precious, dirty, dirty little monkey."

Discarding the sponge into the water, she rubs Pet's small breasts, pinching both erect nipples between her fingers.

"I love your body," she whispers, encouraging Pet to rest against her shoulder. "Every inch of it." She drops one hand below the surface of the water, seeking out Pet's already lengthening augmentation.

Adding this to her ever increasing list of sexual firsts, Pet closes her eyes and enjoys the sensation as Coralie begins stroking her rising erection. Once she's certain she has her anatomical response to Coralie's touch under control, and is at no risk of embarrassing herself, she arches her back and reaches behind her, fumbling for Coralie's core. It's not the most conducive angle for a decent fuck, but she receives a whimper of sincere appreciation when the tip of her middle finger grazes Coralie's swollen clit.

"Let's make each other come." Coralie chews on Pet's earlobe. "I haven't had a release in almost twenty-four hours. I think I'm going to pop."

Harnessing every bit of concentration that isn't already dedicated to the task of holding back her own climax, Pet focuses on the action of her hand, swirling her fingers around the hard nub at the apex of Coralie's sex. Her eyes still closed, she listens to Coralie's breathing, paying attention to every whine, working on increasing their frequency until Coralie is a shivering, moaning wreck.

When it's time, Coralie's usual command for completion doesn't even make it out of her mouth. She gets as far as "Come—" and her words dissolve into a cry of two-fold pleasure, a powerful orgasm coursing through her as Pet's erection swells and erupts in her hand.

Afterward, sparing a few minutes to remember how to breathe, Pet squirms around and plants a kiss on Coralie's lips. Now face to face, she finds Coralie's breast beneath a mound of bubbles and clutches it, tweaking the nipple she had her lips around last night and giving it a slight tug, massaging and pulling on it, testing for a reaction.

Coralie chuckles. "If you're hoping for a treat, you'll need to wait until the sun sets." She stays Pet's hand. "Plus, I'm a little sore from last night." She switches Pet over to her other breast. "You suck hard, and you have sharp teeth."

Pet lets her hand fall away, her expression turning instantly apologetic.

"It's all right." Coralie puts her hand back. "Ordinarily, I love it when you bite my nipples, but I think I've discovered that twenty full minutes of it is a bit much. And I can't just wave my hand and make it all better. It would be a violation of coven law to use my magic on myself."

On that note, Pet taps her lips, indicating her wish to speak.

"Okay, talk to me, Pet." Coralie sweeps her arm around Pet's waist. "But only if you're about to say something incredibly flattering." She holds up a mock finger of warning.

"I was wondering ..." Pet rubs her thumb over Coralie's tender nipple, mustering the confidence to ask, "Have you ... last night ... with other ... ?"

Coralie shakes her head. "Only you, my love. It seemed far too intimate a delight to share with anyone but my bonded companion." She instigates a kiss. "I suppose you could say that I was saving myself for you."

Given Coralie's history of promiscuity, that's a giggle-worthy notion, but Pet's still visibly relieved to know that she gets to share something with Coralie—even if it's just one small thing—that no-one else will ever have.

"I've never been this happy," she states for the record, caressing Coralie's soft skin. "I didn't even know I could be."

"Nor did I." Coralie sighs contentedly. "You really are perfect." She explores Pet's body with her eyes. "So absolutely, completely perfect." She draws Pet to her chest. "Thank you for indulging me in the car, by the way. I know I said I'd never force myself on you, but your anatomy was so responsive, and—"

Pet plants another kiss on her, silencing her apology. "I liked it."

"Did you?" Coralie captures her lips again. "I wasn't too aggressive?"

"I trust you."

As Pet repositions for comfort, Coralie feels something stiff jabbing at her pubic mound.

"Unfortunately, I don't think we have time for that." She holds Pet off. "We need to get out of this tub before we turn all pruny."

Pet grumbles, but heaves herself up and out, then helps Coralie out after her. Instead of drying themselves, they dry each other, Coralie taking extra care to rub behind Pet's ears and around her collar, leaving no inch untended. Once done, Coralie slips into some clean underwear and slinks over to the vanity in the bedroom. She's about to start moisturizing her legs when Pet, still nude, crawls up to her and volunteers herself for the task instead.

"Have I mentioned how devastatingly perfect you are?" Coralie leans back on the vanity chair, propping her leg up to give Pet better access. "I should be the one worshipping you."

Pet blushes, working the cream between Coralie's toes before moving upward, dropping kisses all over her thighs in the process.

"You know you'll have to stay with me tonight." Coralie crooks her other leg over Pet's shoulder. "There's nowhere for you to retreat."

Pet nods, but makes no comment, her kisses making their way to Coralie's crotch.

"Oh, naughty, Pet." Coralie pulls Pet's face away, displaying a wet spot in the gusset of her knickers. "Look at what you've done to me." She trails a finger along her cleft. "How can I go back downstairs reeking of lust?"

Pet opens her mouth to respond, but Coralie puts a finger to her lips.

"Hush." She tenders Pet a kiss. "No more talking." She pushes Pet's head back down. "Clean up the mess you've made."

CHAPTER ELEVEN

WHILE CORALIE APPLIES A FRESH COAT OF MAKEUP IN THE bedroom, Pet sits alone in the bathroom, concentrating hard, trying to temporarily banish her priapus. If only to prevent further embarrassments with it, she wants to be in control of the thing.

To that end, determined to get to grips with her complex anatomy, she closes her eyes and wishes it away. When that doesn't work, she stares at the flaccid rod in a threatening manner, hoping to frighten it off. No such luck. Pleading with it doesn't help, either.

Growing exasperated with her failure to affect change—unable to generate even the faintest tingle in her loins—she takes a deep breath, closes her eyes again, and tries a different approach. This time, instead of focusing all her energy on driving away her augmentation, she tries to coax out her vagina by recalling how it felt when Coralie's mouth was on her.

The heat.

Her probing tongue.

Soft lips.

All the sucking ... the licking ...

She remembers Coralie's finger sliding into her, swirling around in her depths, and a warmth spreads throughout her abdomen. Half opening one eye, she peers down at her crotch, breaking into a victorious grin to see the return of her girl parts.

Eager to share her good news with Coralie, she bounds into the bedroom and leaps onto the four-poster, grinning from ear to ear and bouncing up and down.

"My love!" Coralie giggles at her antics. "Why so rambunctious?"

Pet kneels on the edge of the bed, pointing to her crotch.

"Ah, you've been practicing." Coralie rises to congratulate her. "See, I told you it was possible." She pecks Pet's nose and reaches a hand between her legs, surprised to find her flesh slick with arousal. "Gods, you're so wet." She gasps. "Whatever were you thinking about in there?"

Blushing furiously, Pet takes hold of Coralie's wrist and directs her gentle fingers toward the inner pink, suggesting the penetrative nature of her imaginings.

"Mmm, such delicious thoughts." Coralie teases the entrance to her body. "Is this what you want?" She dips a finger inside. "Do you want me to fuck you, Pet?"

Without waiting for a response, she eases in another finger, stretching Pet's hymen, the sudden intrusion causing the young companion to flinch.

"Try to relax." Coralie wraps her arm around Pet's waist, gripping her firmly. "I want to break you in." She persists, despite Pet's minor discomfort. "Will you let me?"

Pet nods, not entirely sure she knows what that entails.

"Thank you, Pet." Coralie releases her. "Now lie down."

Pinching her lower lip between her teeth, Pet does as she's told, silently offering herself to her Mistress, while Coralie pulls open the drawer in the bedside table and withdraws a modest seven-inch dildo, followed by a leather harness. In a flash, she wriggles into the contraption, secures it around her hips, and douses the cock in lubricant, preparing it for use.

Pet forgets to breathe. Coralie looks quite a sight, standing there by the bedside wearing bra, stockings, and cock, and she can't help but stare aghast at the protruding phallus, her insides clenching at the thought of being pierced by it.

"It might hurt at first," Coralie addresses the concerned look on her face as she clambers onto the bed. "Just a little." She maneuvers between Pet's legs and leans over her, pinning her there. "But pleasure will soon follow, I promise." She pushes the head through Pet's labia, nudging it up against her slit. "Now talk to me, darling. Tell me you want this."

Pet mewls, peering down at the junction of their bodies.

"Tell me," Coralie insists sternly. "Else I shan't do it." She begins to back away, the connection about to be lost, but Pet clutches her buttocks.

"Fuck me," she whispers, urging Coralie to her cunt. "Please."

Coralie dips down to kiss her, letting the dildo slither its way back to her obstructed opening, bumping against her clit before it slips lower and hits the mark. When she feels it's in position—the resistance of Pet's hymen barring her way—she gives a short, sharp thrust, forcing the mushroom-shaped head in up to the crown. In that moment, Pet's body gives way to her, the barrier broken in one fell swoop.

Trained not to complain, Pet doesn't squeal. She merely winces, turning her head to obscure the traces of pain she can't hide. Fortunately, the worst is over with and Coralie forges on, gliding the smooth shaft all the way in without any further difficulty.

"You're not a virgin in any way now, Pet." She keeps her movements slow and languid, hyperaware of the tension in Pet's body. "How does it feel this time?"

Still recovering from the initial sting of defloration, Pet grasps Coralie's breasts and murmurs softly, incapable of forming words. Hoping to increase her pleasure, Coralie changes the angle of her thrust, targeting a spongy button of skin deep inside Pet's sex and keeping the pressure there until she lets out a phenomenal moan.

"Good, Pet." Coralie concentrates her efforts. "Come for me."

In the next second, Pet gushes all over Coralie, her body responding to the command, regardless of the recent changes to her anatomy. Her ejaculation horrifies her, but it makes Coralie ecstatic.

"I guess you come in torrents no matter what parts you have." She chuckles.

"I'm sorry." Pet grimaces at the mess she's made. "I didn't mean to do that!"

"Nonsense!" Coralie bursts into a broad grin. "It was perfect, and I take full credit for teaching your body to ejaculate on cue."

Pet whines as Coralie pulls out, bracing herself as the fat head pops free and causes another sting of pain. In the aftermath, she slips a hand over her burning, throbbing sex and explores it for the first time, investigating the tender skin surrounding her opening, dismayed to then find her fingertips smeared pink: a mixture of blood and sex.

"It's not unusual to bleed a little the first time," Coralie assures her, not knowing how well she's ever been educated about matters of sex. "And besides"—she unfastens the harness, dropping it to the floor—"I can make it all better." She ducks down, kissing away the injury.

In a post-orgasmic glow, Coralie skips down the main staircase with Pet in tow behind her. Awaiting her arrival, the other Mistresses are milling around in the hall, preparing to lock themselves away in the High Council chamber to conduct their monthly business—from which the companions are excluded.

"You're late." Mistress Diana checks her watch.

"We were rather busy," Coralie boasts unapologetically, adjusting her bra inside her fresh, pristine suit. "Pet can't keep her hands off me."

Out of habit—one that surfaces particularly in the presence of other Mistresses—Pet tucks herself behind Coralie's shoulder, slyly demonstrating her affection by placing a hand on the small of her back: an intimate but subtle touch.

Regrettably, now's the time they must part company. The wide double doors open on the parlor: a place for the companions to gather while the Mistresses are convened in the High Council chamber. In this room, and this room only, the companions can communicate without boundaries or fear of reproach—no permission required. Some companions use this time to revisit old friendships, engaging in light foreplay. Nudity is optional.

It's standard procedure for the Mistresses to drop their companions off here, but Mistress Isabelle, fearful of gossip, never allowed Pet anywhere near the parlor. Forbidden from socializing with the other companions, Pet was isolated and alone, left tethered in the hallway for hours on end. And to a point, that suited her just fine.

Chronically shy, she clings to Coralie's arm, shaking her head, genuinely terrified by the prospect of being trapped in a room with her peers. Once inside, no companion can leave until her Mistress returns, and Pet can't conceive of anything worse than spending the afternoon with a gaggle of other women who've most likely, at some time or another, had various parts of their anatomy buried inside Coralie.

"Go," Coralie insists, nudging her toward the doorway. "I hate to think of you sitting all by yourself. Wouldn't you rather be among friends? People you can talk freely with."

She tries to pry Pet away from her, but Pet grips her waist, holding onto her for dear life. She can feel Pet's tiny fists clenched around her blouse, pulling the silky fabric taut around her midsection, threatening to pop a button at her bust.

Sensing the need for a little leniency on account of Pet's obvious misgivings, Coralie decides to make a deal with her. "I'll come check on you in an hour or so. If you're not having any fun, I'll take you out and you can wait for me in our bedroom. How does that sound?" She strokes Pet's shoulders. "Am I being fair?"

Pet nods, reminding herself how lucky she is to have a Mistress who considers her feelings, even when they're founded in absurd fears.

"That's settled, then." Coralie smiles and pats her bum. "Off you trot now."

Pet turns to leave, but her insecurities get the better of her. Needing just a little more courage, she stands on her tippy-toes, flings her arms around Coralie's neck, and crushes her pink lips to Coralie's crimsons.

As promised, her advance is met with nothing short of full reciprocation, the meeting of tongues lasting for as long as Coralie lets it, the gratuitous display garnering nothing but disapproval from any other Mistresses within eyeshot.

"All right, that's enough." Coralie extricates herself from Pet's grasp. "You have to go."

Just to clarify, Pet holds up her index finger, both eyebrows raised, hoping for a more solid pledge that Coralie intends to return to her in precisely one hour.

"Yes, my love." Coralie boops her nose. "One hour. I swear it." She spins Pet toward the parlor and gives her a gentle shove. "Now enjoy."

Pet breaches the room under severe duress, calling to mind at least a thousand other places she'd rather be at this moment. Never particularly sociable at the best of times, arriving late to the parlor to find the rest of the companions already settled in their cliques is the epitome of her worst nightmares.

She's the odd one out. Having never been in the coterie, she didn't get to meet any of these companions back when they were playmates, and since this is the first time she's ever set foot in the parlor, it's also the first time she's ever been in a position to engage any of them in conversation. It's daunting, and they're not exactly being welcoming.

Most of them are familiar to her, of course. She's seen them with their Mistresses in the dining hall, and at other moments during past gatherings. In fact, some of them are rather more familiar to her than she'd like.

She spots Brat across the room, but has no interest in initiating any social contact. All she can picture is Coralie on the drawing room floor, being fucked hard and fast from behind, and the recollection makes her chest ache. Cringing, she looks away, seeking a quiet place to sit by herself and count down the minutes until Coralie returns.

The parlor itself is decked out like a playroom. Seating is split between couches and beanbags, with board games and gaming systems scattered all around. There are books, magazines, and a table full of snack foods and soft drinks.

Sticking to the outskirts of the room, Pet finds an unoccupied beanbag and plonks into it, curling herself up into a ball. As soon as the doors are closed, conversations spark up and she hopes to be ignored, but a busty blonde—newly risen from the coterie and thus a complete stranger to Pet—has other ideas.

With her waistcoat and shirt unbuttoned, her unfettered breasts on display, she strides purposefully across the room, digging a packet of cigarettes and a lighter out of her back pocket.

"So you're the one." She drops cross-legged to the floor in front of Pet's beanbag.

"The one what?" Pet peeks up at her.

"Coralie's new toy."

Pet hugs her knees to her chest, regarding the blonde suspiciously. "Who are you?"

"My name's Fawn." She puts a cigarette to her lips. "I'm your predecessor."

"What?" Pet glowers at her.

"I was with Coralie in the coterie." Fawn lights the cigarette. "I was her favorite."

Pet stays silent. It hadn't occurred to her that Coralie might've had a preferred playmate in the coterie, and she certainly hadn't given any thought to the fact that she might have barged in on a pre-existing relationship.

"It's funny, you don't look that special to me." Fawn sucks on the cigarette. "You're just a wee tiny thing." She grabs Pet's knees and wrenches her legs apart, trying to get a look at her package. "What do you keep in there? A pencil? How're you gonna keep her happy with that?"

Pet kicks Fawn away and retreats further into the safety of the beanbag.

"You know your precious Mistress is a filthy slut, don't you?" Fawn leers over her. "I can't believe she fell for this sweet, sad little girl thing you've got going on."

"Stop it." Pet grits her teeth.

"She used to take all of us." Fawn leans over the beanbag, breathing smoke in Pet's face. "One right after the other, or several of us at once."

On the verge of tears, Pet shakes her head. "I don't want to know."

"She's no Mistress." Fawn sits back on her heels, drawing more smoke into her lungs. "She's just something to be fucked, over and over again."

"Enough!" Brat chimes in, descending on their conversation. "Leave her alone." She rolls Pet over to the other side of the beanbag and squishes in beside her.

Now topless, Brat makes herself comfortable and thieves Fawn's cigarette. "Stop being such a bitch." She takes a puff. "It's not Pet's fault that Mistress Coralie overlooked you in favor of a younger specimen."

"Fuck you." Fawn helps herself to Brat's breasts. "She stole my ticket out of the coterie. I had to put a lot of work in to get cozy with another Mistress after I was ditched."

"I didn't steal anything." Pet colors up at the sight of two women fondling each other right in front of her. "Coralie *chose* me."

"Yeah, why is that exactly?" Brat unfastens her pants, letting Fawn inside. "She didn't even know you. What did you do to get your hands on her?"

Pet shrugs. "I didn't do anything. I just ... I loved her as soon as I saw her."

Fawn laughs, her face busy in Brat's crotch. "Love?!"

"I love her, and she loves me back," Pet insists.

"Does she?" Fawn sits up and wipes her lips. "Has she ever told you that?"

Suddenly, unable to recall that Coralie ever has, Pet looks a lot less sure of herself.

"She's just like the rest of them." Brat brushes it off. "Don't be fooled, and don't give it another thought." She flings her arm out, her hand landing on Pet's leg. "Anyway, now that you're away from the old witch, how about having some fun with us?" She makes a bid for Pet's crotch. "Let's see what you're hiding in here ..."

"No!" Pet swipes her hand away. "That's not for you!"

"Whatever." Brat returns her attention to Fawn, massaging the erection she's now sporting. "Are you gonna fuck me? Or just tease me?"

"I'm gonna fuck you." Fawn flips her over onto her stomach and yanks down her jeans, lifting her hips up. "Just the way you like it."

For Pet, time couldn't possibly move fast enough. Brat and Fawn enjoy each other next to her on the beanbag, so close she can hear every squelch and splurge. At one point, Fawn slams into Brat so hard that Brat falls forward, becoming wedged between Fawn and the beanbag, no freedom to move. To Pet's eye, it looks like it should hurt. Fawn's priapus is stretching Brat to the very limit of what ought to be comfortable, yet Brat takes it with relish, screaming for more.

And more.

And more.

When the parlor doors finally open and Coralie walks in, all conversation and sex play grinds to a halt. The room falls respectfully silent in the presence of a Mistress, and Pet leaps off the beanbag, dashing to greet her, colliding into her when she's barely through the door.

"Pet!" Coralie giggles, struggling to stay on her feet under the force of her lover's hug. "Such enthusiasm! I was only gone for an hour."

Dropping to her knees, Pet lifts Coralie's skirt and covers her thighs with kisses, causing her to stumble backwards into the wall.

"Did you miss me?" Coralie strokes the back of her head.

Pet whines into her flesh.

"Good, Pet." Coralie grabs a fistful of her mane and tilts her head back. "I missed you, too." She pulls fretful Pet to her feet. "So what's the verdict?"

Pet shoves her face in Coralie's bosom and holds her tight: She doesn't want to be left in the parlor a minute longer.

"Very well." Coralie leads her to the door. "I'll take you to bed."

On the way out, she feels another pair of eyes watching her and glances back into the room, catching a very naked, very erect Fawn glaring at her.

Masking her shock to see that Fawn's managed to attach herself to another Mistress so soon—her eyes glowing with the distinctive fire of a bonded companion, which was probably the result of some magical underhandedness—Coralie returns the glare. Seconds before the parlor doors close, she makes sure the last thing Fawn gets an eyeful of is a passionate kiss between Mistress and companion, then she hurries Pet upstairs, lavishing more kisses on her as soon as they get inside their bedroom.

"You stay here and wait for me." She moans into another lip-lock, finding it difficult to tear herself away. "I'll be back soon." She sucks Pet's lower lip into her mouth. "You'll be okay by yourself?" One more kiss. "I hate leaving you alone."

She can tell something's wrong—Pet's kisses are weak—but she doesn't press. She has to get back to the High Council chamber, and Pet doesn't look as though she's in the mood to talk. So, with some reluctance, she pecks Pet's forehead and leaves her to her own devices, proceeding then to spend the next several hours unable to hold a single thought without concern for her young companion seeping in.

CHAPTER TWELVE

At the close of the high council session, when the Mistresses are finally released to prepare for dinner, Coralie practically flies up to the stairs to Pet. In the mood for a few stolen moments of intimacy before getting zipped into the brand new evening dress she let Pet pick out for her last week, she breezes into the bedroom and kicks off her stilettos, hoping to find her young lover restored. Sadly, that's not to be the case.

"Are you hungry, Pet?" She strips to her underwear. "I'm starving, and I can't wait to—" She stops herself.

Pet's lying in bed, sobbing hysterically, the duvet bunched around her heaving shoulders.

"Oh, my darling." Coralie crawls onto the four-poster. "Don't be so upset." She extends a hand to the quivering bundle of pink flesh before her. "Whatever's wrong? Talk to me."

Pet sniffles and chokes, having worked herself up into a blubbering, slobbery mess incapable of speech or coherent thought.

"I'm here now." Coralie kisses her hair, soothing her. "Tell me what troubles you."

Fearing the worst about Coralie's true feelings for her—or the lack thereof—and having had plenty of time to stew on it since being pulled out of the parlor, Pet lays her heart bare, hoping to hear something reassuring in return.

"I love you," she croaks, trying to get her tears under control, the confession setting off another pitiful wail.

Compounding her misery, nothing comforting is immediately forthcoming, and in the protracted silence that follows, she grows fearful, her breathing abated until she feels Coralie's warm body spoon up behind her.

"I love you, Pet." Coralie slips an arm around her waist. "More than anything." She wriggles under the duvet, discovering that Pet's not wearing any pants. "Were you afraid that I didn't? Is that what this is about?"

Pet mumbles something unintelligible.

"Sweetheart, I've loved you since the first time we kissed." Coralie hooks her leg over Pet's hip, molding their bodies together. "Don't ever doubt that."

"Why didn't you tell me?"

"My precious darling, you've been so overwhelmed by everything. The first night I took you home, you cried for two hours because I invited you to sit on the sofa. The following morning, we showered together for the first time and you came all over me as I soaped your cute little body."

"I got it in your eye." Pet pulls a face, remembering the incident well.

"Accidents happen." Coralie laughs. "The point is, I couldn't tell you I loved you. You weren't ready to hear it, and I didn't want you to feel obligated to return the sentiment, or feel bad because you couldn't." She holds Pet to her chest. "Now, let's get to the bottom of all these silly tears. What happened in the parlor? Did the other companions say something to set this off? Did they upset you?"

Pet snivels into her pillow. "I met Fawn."

"She's the one who made you feel this way?" Coralie infers. "I should've guessed."

"She told me she was your favorite." Pet wipes her nose on her sleeve and rolls onto her back, looking up at Coralie. "Why didn't you choose her when you ascended?"

"A few reasons." Coralie dries Pet's teary face. "The most relevant of which is lying in this bed with me right now." She gives her lover a soft kiss. "So was that the only thing bothering you? Or dare I ask, is there more?"

Pet shrugs. "Is it true that you had all the playmates?" She looks sheepish. "And ... together? Like, at the same time."

"I wish I could say no." Coralie draws Pet to her bosom. "I'm sorry."

"I don't want to share you." Pet weeps into her cleavage, soaking her bra.

"You don't have to." Coralie cradles her, rocking her back and forth. "Ever."

"You don't miss the coterie?"

"Not even a teensy weensy little bit." Coralie lifts Pet's head up. "You satisfy my every desire. Making love to you feels more incredible than I ever could've imagined."

"You're being kind." Pet takes the compliment with a grain of salt. "Sometimes, I'm not so good." She sighs forlornly. "I know I'm not, but I can't help it. You feel so amazing, and when I'm in you, I just ..."

"Sshhh." Coralie grins. "We've been together less than two months. If you didn't get a tad over-excited every now and then, I think I'd be a little insulted."

Pet attempts a small laugh, her lingering despondency soon erasing it.

"Do you like being a companion, Pet?" Coralie digs deeper into her insecurities. "Being *my* companion especially?"

"I *love* you." Pet's hand finds Coralie's stockinged leg beneath the covers. "Of course I like being your companion. Why would you ask me that?"

"I see a look in your eyes sometimes." Coralie studies her face, captivated by her beautiful, bright irises. "You seem so afraid. Does it still intimidate you to be with me?"

"I've never done this before." Pet bites back another flood of tears. "Until you, I never knew what it was like to be touched or kissed. I'd never—"

"Wait," Coralie cuts her off. "Mistress Isabelle didn't even kiss you?"

Pet snorts. "The only part of me Mistress Isabelle had any interest in was my thing-um-bob, and I think she'd have liked that much better if it'd been attached to a man. There was no kissing, no caressing, and when she wanted me to touch her, she always closed her eyes. She was as much repulsed by me as I was by her."

"Huh." Coralie mulls on that. "No wonder she was so miserable all the time. If that was her problem all along, she should've chosen a coven that was better suited to her particular proclivities. We don't care for men. Hence the need for this." She wraps her hand around Pet's soft priapus.

"Maybe she didn't have a choice," Pet contends. "I know I didn't."

Coralie's brow creases. "How old were you when you were groomed for the coterie?"

"Twelve."

"So young." She cups Pet's peachy face. "That's not how things are usually done. You were just a little girl. Most are older, and they've already established their sexual identities. They *want* this life, but you were practically raised for it. Your parents consented to this?"

"I never had any," Pet discloses casually, the pain dulled by the passage of time. "I was found in an orphanage. When they got sick of me, the coven took me. No questions asked."

"Siblings?"

Pet shakes her head. "I never had anyone. The coven took me, put this on me"—she loops a finger through the ring on her collar—"and gave me the thing-um-bob. They told me I would serve a Mistress one day, and that my purpose was to breed."

"Oh, my love." Coralie's heart breaks for her. "What about men?"

"What about them?" Pet screws up her face.

"Well, are you gay?" Coralie asks flatly. "Do you even know?"

"What difference does it make? Do you doubt that I want to be with you?" If Pet had any tears left to cry, they'd be streaming down her cheeks. "I've never met anyone like you. I feel so safe with you, and I want to spend the rest of my life with you."

"But—"

"What is there but?" Pet scowls indignantly at her.

"I don't know." Coralie shrugs. "I suppose I'd just like to be sure that, given the choice, you'd still choose this life over one free from the coven."

"I would now," Pet assures her. "But I don't think my purpose is to breed." She pauses, thinking of all the changes that have taken place in her life over the last few weeks. "I believed that for a long time, but I don't think it's so true anymore."

"No?" Coralie tries and fails to hide her concern. "I thought last night you said—"

"Let me finish." Pet plants a kiss on her worried lips, grinning. "I think now that my purpose is to love you."

Tears well in Coralie's eyes. "You know, I was taught that it shows great weakness to demonstrate genuine affection for one's companion. Among the Mistresses, power and strength is linked directly to fertility. The more children I bear, the more I shall be respected, and in that process, companions are intended to be a means to an end."

Some of Pet's insecurity returns, but Coralie swiftly quashes it.

"I never felt that way." She unbuttons Pet's snot-smeared shirt. "I want so desperately to sit at the head of the High Council table, but not alone." She reaches the bottom of the shirt and tugs it open. "I've never wanted to live my life void of love, or passion, or tenderness." Her hands roam over Pet's body. "I've always wanted a companion—a *real* companion—and I have that with you, Pet. None of this means anything without you." She sits up, grabbing Pet's open shirt and pulling her into a kiss. "I love you." She slips the shirt off Pet's shoulders. "We wouldn't be here if I didn't."

Pet wriggles out of her clothing and throws it to the floor, diving back to Coralie's lips with renewed fervor. Lying breast to breast with her paramour, she draws

Coralie's leg over her hip, their tongues and limbs entwined, their bodies rocking together.

Breaking for air, Coralie picks Pet's hand off her waist and puts it on her breast. "Are you thirsty?" She unhooks her bra. "Want something to drink?"

Pet's priapus rises.

"I'll take that as a yes." Coralie giggles, casting off her lingerie. "I've been looking forward to this all day." She massages her virgin breast, her other nipple still sore. "I'm aching for you." She teases out a drop of milk. "Come to me."

She guides Pet to her breast, murmuring softly when Pet's mouth engulfs her nipple, and again when Pet's erection slips between her thighs, sliding along her cleft.

The dual stimulation is unparalleled. Between Pet's vigorous manipulation of her breast—tugging, sucking, biting, squeezing—and the continuous, rhythmic humping of Pet's turgid anatomy, she climaxes in under five minutes.

"Mmm, darling." Coralie breaks Pet's suction and holds her off. "Maybe we should stop before we get too carried away. You're making me so wet."

"I'm leaking, too." Pet directs her gaze down, showing her a slimy bridge of milky fluid connecting their bodies. "Anyway, I don't want to stop." She rolls on top of Coralie, resuming her gentle humping.

"But we can't." Coralie whimpers, staring out the window. "The moon is already up."

Pet's stiffness probes between her labia, kept at bay only by the thin, gauzy strip of sodden fabric that's masquerading as the gusset of her knickers.

"I know." Pet strips off the undies, tearing them down Coralie's long legs.

Thinking this is much too good to be true, Coralie thrusts out her hand, grabbing Pet's rigid, in-no-way-deflating priapus, finding it not just rock hard, but also far more swollen than she's ever felt it before.

"Gods, how big are you?!" She pushes on Pet's chest, forcing her upright so that she can get a better look at the monster she's about to be impaled with. "You're huge!"

"I don't know why it's like that." Pet frowns at her turgid anatomy.

"I do." Coralie is glowing. "It's the moon."

"Will it even fit?" Pet nestles the engorged purple head in Coralie's tiny slit. "I don't want to hurt you."

"You won't." Coralie watches it push at the entrance to her body. "I promise."

Putting her faith in Coralie's assessment of the task at hand, Pet forces herself in. She pops the crown through and stretches Coralie open, generating a drawn-out, voluptuous moan.

"I've never been so filled." Coralie gasps, tilting her pelvis to better accommodate Pet's invasion of her body. "You're divine."

Once the enormous head is safely inserted, Pet feeds her another few inches, watching her face for any trace of discomfort. "Is it too much?" She holds back.

"No." Coralie grabs her bum, urging her deeper. "I want it all."

Pet advances another inch, finding that there's one distinct drawback to her enhanced size: they fit together much too snugly. As she slides fully into Coralie's heat, hilting herself in a single stroke, the sensations become too intense. It's like her first time all over again, and it isn't long before the inevitable pressure boils in her abdomen.

"I'm sorry," she rasps, rapidly losing control. "I can't last."

"Don't be sorry." Coralie groans every time Pet hits bottom, feeling as though she's being lanced by a hot steel rod. "Come for me."

Upon hearing those words, Pet's training causes her to erupt into Coralie's fertile womb. Her body shaking, she comes so hard she forgets to breathe, her head spinning and her heart pounding. And that's not all she has to offer. She withdraws halfway, confirming that she's lost none of her length and girth, her ability to perform not in the least bit reduced by her orgasm.

"Keep giving it to me," Coralie encourages her, reading her mind. "As many times as you can, for as long as you can."

That turns out to be quite the request. Pet starts moving again, and the second time around, she lasts for a full ten minutes. The third time, it's twenty. For the fourth, she makes it to thirty and takes Coralie in every position she can think of, and for the finale—the fifth and final round—she goes for almost an hour. Her last ejaculation isn't nearly as powerful as the first, but the moment shared between them is no less passionate.

Both thoroughly exhausted, Pet's augmentation finally softening, they uncouple for the last time and Coralie flops onto her back, breathing hard.

"Wow." She snuggles closer to Pet. "Just ... wow."

"I don't know what's wrong with me." Pet pants, her priapus sore, raw from the friction.

"Nothing's wrong with you, darling." Coralie nurses her aching cunt. "Your body's just trying to make sure we have the best chance of conceiving. It's perfectly natural." She reconsiders that. "Well, I mean, it might not exactly be natural, but it's completely normal for a companion." She reaches out to hold Pet's hand. "Until now, I'd never had sex on a moon night—it was forbidden—but I knew it was bound to be exceptional."

"I did okay?" Pet wipes her deflating, still dripping anatomy on the duvet, wincing as the fabric grates her hyper-sensitive skin like sandpaper.

"You did brilliantly." Coralie sweeps her hand lightly over Pet's aching crotch, relieving the discomfort in her tender loins. "But as much as I would love to lie here with you and marinate in your virility, we really must get dressed, else we'll be late for dinner."

Pet tries to move, but her legs are like jelly. "How long before I can please you again?" she wonders aloud, her mind already leaping ahead to their next bout of epic lovemaking.

"Not long." Coralie swoons over her, so pleased with this sudden turn around. "We'll get some food in you, and you'll be restored in no time."

"And how long before I'll be able to feel my toes?" Pet wiggles her feet.

Giggling, Coralie reaches over and presses her palm to Pet's middle, sending a jolt of energy through every cell in her body, returning normal sensation to her limbs and alleviating the inflammation in her overworked muscles.

"I wish I could do what you do." Pet mewls, simultaneous heat and chills bombarding her senses. "Do all the Mistresses have your touch?"

Coralie shakes her head. "Every Mistress has a unique gift. It first presents when we blossom, and grows stronger year by year."

"Blossom?"

"Come of age," she explains. "We're all born the same way, with latent magic." She whispers her fingertips over Pet's lily white skin. "I can't change who I am. I was destined for this life from the time I was conceived, but you weren't. You could still be a normal eighteen-year-old girl … if you wanted to be."

"How?" Pet wraps her hand around her collared neck. "Not with this."

"No, but your collar could be stripped," Coralie enlightens her. "It's possible. There are many ways you could violate coven law, and the punishment would be automatic."

"Then I wouldn't be your companion anymore." Pet turns forlorn.

"I'd still love you." Coralie smiles sadly. "The collar is symbolic of our commitment to one another, but it has no influence over my heart. That's not magic, it's real."

"But we wouldn't be together." Tears pool in Pet's eyes.

Coralie shakes her head. "For as long as I'm fertile, I'm obligated to take a companion."

"So what'd happen to me?" Pet's chest tightens, anxiety creeping in. "Where would I go? Would I ever see you again?"

Coralie's silence says it all.

CHAPTER THIRTEEN

FOR ALL THEIR BEST EFFORTS TO ARRIVE AT THE DINNER table on time, Coralie and Pet are still the last pair to take their places in the dining room of the High Council, settling in opposite the seat formerly occupied by Mistress Isabelle.

Of course, that chair wasn't vacant for long. Replacing Pet's boozy former bond is a young, redheaded Mistress who's no stranger to Coralie. Ascended early by virtue of her bloodline—as Coralie did when her aunt Alessa died—Mistress Liora already has a bonded companion by her side.

It's Fawn.

Doing her best to ignore the vicious glances thrown her way by her disgruntled former coterie favorite, Coralie smiles flirtatiously at Liora.

"Welcome to the table." She adjusts the neckline of her black velvet dress. "I must say, I'd grown accustomed to that cute face of yours." She dishes food onto Pet's plate. "Admittedly, I'm used to seeing it buried between my legs, but I'm sure I'll adjust."

No sooner have the words left her lips than she feels a warm hand creep onto her lap. Covering that hand with her own, she looks down and gives Pet a furtive wink.

"Come here." She holds her arms open, inviting Pet to rise up from her cushion and lean in for a cuddle. "Let me feed you."

Keen to put on a display in front of the other Mistresses, Pet sprawls over Coralie's lap, paws to thighs and cheek to breast. She accepts food from Coralie's hand, and kisses from her lips at intervals, their closeness provoking Mistress Diana's wrath.

"Your companion's place is on the floor, not in your lap."

"My companion's place is as close to me as she can be," Coralie replies sharply. "If she wishes to drape herself over my lap and nuzzle my breast, then so she shall."

Tempting fate, Coralie inflames Diana further by feeding Pet from her own plate, and sharing a fork with her, no less.

"Enough!" Diana slams the butt of her knife down on the table, making several of the other Mistresses jump.

She grumbles something about proper conduct and returns to her food, while Pet sinks back to her cushion, retreating to a more appropriate position on the floor. On the way down, she notices that Fawn has disappeared from view, lying on her cushion instead of sitting on it.

Curious to know what Fawn's doing down there, Pet drops lower and peers beneath the table, catching Fawn eyeing Coralie's legs. Instinctively, she growls, warning Fawn off, but the signal of her displeasure has little noticeable effect.

Upon hearing it, however, Coralie touches a hand to Pet's mane. "Pet." She bends to kiss the top of her companion's head, whispering, "You've nothing to be jealous of, my love."

That seems to quiet things down for a moment, but halfway through the dessert course, Coralie squeals and giggles, feeling the delightful tickle of hands on her ankles.

"Pet!" She twists in her chair, expecting to find Pet with a mischievous grin, her wandering paws concealed by the tablecloth.

But Pet hasn't moved an inch. She's sitting on her cushion, both hands in view, perplexed by Coralie's sudden burst of laughter. Realization doesn't dawn until

Coralie's expression turns sour, her jaw clenched, a fleeting glimpse of anger passing across her eyes, then Pet dives back down to the floor, snarling beneath the table.

In response, Fawn—still encroaching far too close to Coralie for Pet's liking—snorts derisively, meeting Pet at the center of the narrow passage.

"Suck my cock," she barks in Pet's ear.

Tableside, the sound of something hard smacking into the woodwork precedes a yelp and a scuffle of hands and feet.

"What in the gods names is going on down there?!" Diana bellows, directing her fury at Coralie. "Control your untethered companion!"

"Perhaps Mistress Liora ought to learn how to control hers!" Coralie slides her chair back and stands up, tossing her napkin onto her plate and stepping away from the table. "Come, Pet."

She issues her command calmly but firmly, patting her outer thigh to convey her second instruction: Heel.

"Excuse us." She starts toward the door, issuing her apology to no-one in particular. "We need to get some air. We'll see you all in the drawing room after dinner."

Catching up, Pet darts around her and opens the door for her, following her out into the hall, and from there, to the drawing room.

Uncharacteristically quiet, Coralie turns her back on Pet. She leans on a sideboard at the edge of the room, hiding her face, and takes a deep breath, shaking with restrained anger.

Thinking she's simply too irate to speak, Pet sidles up to her, ready to grovel at her feet and beg forgiveness. Instead, she's shocked and troubled to find tears spilling down Coralie's face, afraid that she's the cause.

"It's not your fault, darling." Coralie promptly allays her unease. "Everything's fine."

Pet would query that, if she could.

"It's just that wretched—" Coralie stops herself and takes a deep breath, deciding against wasting her anger on Fawn. "You have no idea what she's done, that's all."

She stems the flow of her tears. "I'm sorry I'm such a mess."

Pet taps her mouth, indicating she wants to talk, but Coralie shakes her head.

"Not here. I don't want to be overheard." She dabs at her eyes, careful not to smudge her eye makeup. "We'll talk later, yes? I'll tell you everything. I'll answer all your questions."

Never having seen Coralie cry, Pet is at a loss. Not knowing quite how to proceed in a situation such as this, she reaches up and touches a finger to Coralie's mascara-coated eyelashes, displacing some tears there, mopping them up and restoring perfection.

For that, she receives a small smile, emboldening her to continue. So, she stands on her tippy toes and locks her mouth over Coralie's, initiating a deep kiss, her hands on the older woman's hips. Going further at the severe risk of chastisement, she then brings her mouth to Coralie's ear, whispering gingerly ...

"You're so beautiful."

Pulling back from her with a please-forgive-me face, Pet waits fearfully for her to make the next move, whether it be a slap to the face or a livid denunciation, but instead of a fierce reprimand, she gets passion.

Once Coralie recovers from the shock of hearing Pet speak without her consent, she kisses her timorous companion—first lovingly, then frantically. Groping and pulling on each other, they stagger through the room in a clumsy tangle of arms and legs, their lips locked together. In a frenzy, they tumble onto one of the couches, Pet landing squarely on top of Coralie, her priapus squashed between them.

Her stiff priapus.

Her eager priapus.

At the moment of impact, Coralie gasps, pleasantly surprised by Pet's readiness, and she waits not a second in deciding what she wants from it.

"Let's do it." She grabs Pet's belt, unbuckles her, unfastens her pants, and wrenches them down over her hips. "I want you in me." She kicks off her stilettos and wraps her legs around Pet's tiny waist. "Fuck me." She directs Pet's straining erection straight into her unclad cunt. "Give me a baby."

Pet grabs her by the hips and lays hard into her. Any fears she has about being too rough are soon extinguished by the look of pure lust on Coralie's face, so she plunges harder and faster, the tip of her augmentation kissing Coralie's cervix on every upstroke, their bodies slamming together with unrelenting force.

Determined not to finish until she receives the go-ahead to do so, she clenches her teeth, emitting a guttural roar. She can feel an orgasm stirring in Coralie's body, and amid her Mistress's shivers, contractions, and continuous moans, she's struggling to hold back her impending crisis, her shaft milked by the spasms of Coralie's pulsing, throbbing sex.

"Come with me, Pet." Coralie pulls her energetic young companion close. "Now," she whispers. "Come now!"

Pet does as she's told, collapsing on Coralie's chest as she empties herself into the depths of her lover's receptive womb. When it's over, she makes a weak effort to pull out, her thighs like jelly, but Coralie objects.

"Wait." She clamps her hands on Pet's rear, holding her in place and preventing her withdrawal. "Give it time." She keeps her pelvis tilted up, allaying the effects of gravity.

In the wake of their vigorous, impromptu fuck, noises in the hall signal the imminent arrival of the other Mistresses. Though Coralie would be happy to put on an exhibition and remain locked with Pet indefinitely, Pet's anatomy wilts inside her, unable to sustain itself under the looming threat of an audience.

"Are you ready, darling?" Coralie releases her grip on Pet's rump. "Lick me clean."

Keeping her dress hitched up around her hips, she swings her legs off the couch as Pet slides to her knees and lunges forward, lapping up her sex like a cat lapping at a bowl of cream, savoring every drop and purring all the while.

"I love you," Coralie coos, scooping Pet's dark reddish hair out of the way to get a better view of her bobbing head and bright eyes. "I love you so much."

Done mopping up the spillage, Pet opens her mouth to reciprocate the sentiment, but stops herself; she doesn't have permission.

"I know." Coralie grabs her by the collar and pulls her in for a kiss, tasting their sex on her lips. "Now you might want to put that beautiful thing-um-bob of yours away." She tugs Pet's jeans up. "I don't think the other Mistresses deserve to see it."

Mortified, her cheeks on fire, Pet scrambles to get her jeans back on, tucking her wet priapus inside her clothing before the main door to the drawing room swings open and Mistress Diana and her companion walk through it, closely followed by the other Mistresses and their bonds.

"Couldn't wait for the rest of us?" Mistress Diana takes a seat in a chair beside the fireplace, keeping her distance.

"No." Coralie meets Fawn's angry eyes across the room, relishing the opportunity to rub their union in her face. "I wanted her too much."

Suddenly aware that every companion in the room is staring at her immodest Mistress, hoping for a peek, Pet fixes Coralie's crumpled dress, wishing they could go back to bed. The air is thick with the musk of sex. Everyone knows what they did.

Oblivious to her self-consciousness, and happy beyond measure, Coralie keeps Pet on the floor between her thighs. "Is anyone else feeling exceptionally good this evening?"

Sirena plonks down on the couch beside her, champagne in hand. "Not me, but perhaps my mood could be improved if you lend me Pet for a few hours."

"Envious?" Coralie steals the champagne from her and downs it.

"Exceptionally." Sirena loosens the top of her blouse and hitches up her skirt, her arousal evident. "Would you like to watch?" she offers, directing Brat between her legs and demanding that she put mouth to cunt. "It'll be just like old times. Brat's missed you, and so have I."

Coralie appears momentarily tempted, but her wandering mind is brought rapidly back to the present when Pet squeezes her thighs. Looking down, she finds her companion racked with anxiety, fidgeting uncomfortably, her brow creased. She knows that look well, and it has nothing to with any residual agitation Pet might be feeling about Brat.

"Do you have to pee?"

Pet nods urgently.

"All right." Coralie searches for her shoes and excuses herself to Sirena. "Nature calls."

She takes Pet by the hand and leads her out of the drawing room, escorting her down the hall to the washroom where they shared their first paroxysms together.

"Off you go." She pats Pet's bum. "I'll wait here."

Reluctantly leaving Coralie's side, Pet tends to her full bladder. Passing the time until she returns, Coralie wanders through the front room, admiring the portraits. Many of the women—goddesses and Mistresses alike— have been painted with their bellies full and round, childbirth imminent. Feeling a faint twinge in her own abdomen, she rubs her belly, smiling to herself.

"Won't be long now."

Daydreaming about the future, she doesn't hear the footsteps behind her. She has no idea there's anyone else in the room until a pair of hands slips around her waist, giving a brief squeeze before tugging up her dress.

"Oh, Pet!" She bends forward over a side table. "You want more already?"

Parting her legs, she waits for the hot jab of Pet's seemingly invincible augmentation, and takes a sharp draw of breath when both her arms are unexpectedly wrenched behind her and a hand on her back pins her down.

Caught off-guard—not sure if she should be frightened, aroused, or riled—her reaction is delayed. Turning her head and craning her neck, she manages to peep at Pet's reflection in a mirror on the far wall, only ... it's not Pet.

It's Fawn.

"Back the fuck off." Coralie squirms, trying to free herself. "Have you lost your mind?!"

Fawn unfastens her belt.

"You can't be serious?!" Coralie almost laughs. "Stop this!"

Fawn pulls her belt off.

"I'm a Mistress," Coralie reminds her. "If you want to keep your collar, you have no choice but to follow the rules of this coven and obey my order."

"She's already obeying an order." Mistress Liora stands in the doorway, watching everything unfold. "*My* order."

Liora saunters into the room as Fawn binds Coralie's wrists with the belt.

"To what end?" Coralie snarls. "You want a threesome? Is that it? You've got some way of asking." She struggles fruitlessly. "And by the way"—she glares at her former friend—"the answer's no."

"You're presuming you have a choice." Liora steps up to her. "You don't."

"Care to tell me why?" Coralie winces, the leather pinching and scraping her skin.

"You hurt Fawn's feelings." Liora pouts. "You rejected her when you ascended. How do you think that made her feel? After all she's done for you."

Coralie rolls her eyes. "What's that supposed to mean?"

"Don't play the innocent. You know as well as I do that Mistress Alessa's little tumble down the stairs was no accident." Liora leans near Coralie's ear. "She had help."

"Not from me." Coralie huffs. "Fawn pushed her!"

"Exactly," Liora asserts triumphantly, perplexed as to why Coralie isn't gushing with gratitude. "She would've done anything for you, and you cast her aside."

"Is that what you think?" Coralie grimaces. "You think I coerced Fawn to kill my aunt, then spurned her for Pet? You think I used her?" She shakes her head. "I would *never* have asked her to do something like that. Nor did I want her to."

"Oh, spare me the moral outrage." Liora laughs. "If you were truly upset by Fawn's actions, you would've reported her to the High Council."

"I couldn't." Coralie jerks in Fawn's grasp. "I was the one who helped Fawn sneak out of the coterie in the middle of the night. I was the one who wanted to fuck on the High Council table. And I was standing right there when my aunt left her bedroom to look for me, and Fawn gave her a firm shove from the top step." She chokes up. "How would that have looked?"

"It suited you to stay quiet." Liora shows no sympathy for her. "Why can't you just admit that? It's the same reason you didn't report the prussic acid you found in the kitchen the night before Mistress Isabelle died. You did find it, didn't you? I went back for it, but it was gone."

That takes a moment to sink in, cogs whirring in Coralie's brain. "That was you? You poisoned Isabelle? How could you?! She was your mother!"

"Her death didn't seem to bother you that much at the time." Liora challenges the true depth of her indignation. "As I recall, it played into your hand rather well. How else would you have acquired your darling little Pet?"

"I would've found another way," Coralie counters, her eyes tearing. "I was going to petition Diana after dinner. I was going to declare my affection for her and make a plea for her release. I was—"

"Save it." Liora waves a dismissive hand. "I needed a seat at the table, and you wanted Pet. The way I see it, you're my accomplice."

Coralie shakes her head defiantly. "I had no idea who poisoned Isabelle's wine."

"But you *did* know it was poisoned, and you said nothing." Liora smirks. "I'm sure you tell yourself you were thinking only of Pet's wellbeing, but the truth is, you wanted sex—like you always do—and the end justified the means."

141

"Why are we here?" A tear tumbles down Coralie's cheek. "Whatever this is, let's just finish it. You want my silence? I think you know you already have that."

"That's not it." Liora reaches over Coralie's shoulder and fingers Fawn's hair. "As you can see, Fawn and I became favorites after you ascended. I promised her that once I secured my seat on the High Council, not only would I choose her as my companion, but that I'd also make sure she had the chance to give you what you deserve."

"Ha! So you want me dead?" Coralie sneers. "All because I took exception to the murder of my aunt instead of rewarding Fawn for her initiative."

"Oh, lover, Fawn's not going to kill you. She's going to fuck you."

"On a moon night?" Genuine horror creeps into Coralie's voice.

"What's the matter?" Liora feigns puzzlement. "You always wanted Fawn to sire you a child, didn't you? Well, now she's going to."

"Don't be absurd. I'm bonded to Pet." Coralie tries and fails to wrest herself out of Fawn's grip. "I want no-one's child but hers."

"Ah, yes. The perfect love you've been so recklessly flaunting," Liora scoffs at her devotion. "How will she feel, I wonder, to watch your belly grow, filled with another companion's spawn?"

A muted squeak in the doorway betrays Pet's presence there, the terrified companion unable to intervene without a direct order to do so.

Coralie whips to face her. "Pet, c—"

Before Liora can snap at Fawn to shut Coralie up, Fawn's hand is already covering her mouth, preventing her from giving Pet any instruction to assist. Despite that, Pet takes a bold step forward, her heart overriding her training ...

"Oh, no." Liora holds a hand up, stopping her. "You can stay right there, little one. I want you to watch Fawn pollute your dear Mistress."

142

Bound and gagged, Coralie fights to get free, pain shooting through her cranium as she's forced back over the side table, her head slammed onto the mahogany. On the verge of passing out, her vision clouded, the room spinning, she hears the zipper of Fawn's pants followed by the sensation of a groping hand between her legs. Then ... a thud.

The pressure on her wrists is released, the uninvited hand gone. Confused, she pushes herself vertical, using the side table for much needed support. On the floor at her feet: Fawn. Blood is oozing from her temple, her blonde hair covered in the viscous crimson fluid. Standing over her: Pet, holding a brass fireplace poker.

Another thud: Pet drops the poker to the floor, her hands shaking. Before she follows the murder weapon down, Coralie wriggles free from the belt and catches her, holding her tight.

"It's all right." She peppers Pet's head with kisses. "You're brilliant. You're perfect. You're so brave, and I love you so much."

Pet sobs into Coralie's bosom as Liora runs from the room, returning minutes later flanked by the rest of the High Council, Diana at the forefront of the group.

"Well, what have we here?" Diana surveys the scene.

"Don't hurt her." Coralie holds Pet protectively. "She was defending me."

"From what?" Diana upturns both palms.

Coralie knows how unlikely the words sound before they leave her lips, but she says them anyway. "Fawn was going to force herself on me."

"Utter nonsense." Liora folds her arms. "I was loaning Fawn to her. I was going to watch. You know what she's like. Then Pet barged in, in a jealous rage, and attacked my darling Fawn."

"You lying bitch," Coralie growls.

"Who do you believe?" Liora asks Diana directly. "You believe that Coralie was about to be forced? Or that she wanted a quickie threesome and her untethered companion got out of control? Just look at what happened at the dinner table. Pet attacked Fawn for no reason."

Diana only has to mull things over for a few seconds. "I'm sorry." She sets her own companion on Pet. "I've warned you before, Coralie: you have to keep your companion under control at all times."

Pet is summarily wrenched away by Diana's muscular, boyish companion as two other Mistresses restrain Coralie, parting the lovers by force.

"No!" Coralie protests, reaching desperately for Pet, grasping nothing but air. "Please don't do this to her! Don't punish her for loving me!"

Her use of the L word triggers a round of cruel snickers through the group.

"She acted without order and killed another companion." Diana prepares to strip Pet of her collar. "For that, the punishment is expulsion."

Coralie flits her eyes to Pet and gauges her reaction to the news, searching her pained expression for even the slightest hint that such a discharge from the coven might be welcome.

She finds none.

Consumed by fright, Pet shrieks and fights Diana off, desperate to retain her bond to Coralie, and Coralie floods with relief. Satisfied—and gladdened—that Pet's heart truly lies with her, she wastes no further second and calls Diana off.

"You can't strip her," she growls venomously. "To do so would be a gross violation of our coven law."

"How do you suppose that?" Diana snorts.

"Because I'm pregnant." Coralie silences the room with her declaration. "It's a companion's duty to protect her unborn child—at all costs and by any means necessary. Pet did nothing wrong. Whether I requested Fawn's attentions or not is of no consequence in that. She saw a threat to me, and she acted upon it."

Skeptical about this news, Diana summons Coralie near and presses a palm to her stomach, feeling the energy of newly conceived life emanating from within.

"Congratulations," she tenders begrudgingly. "It seems that Pet's earned her place."

"Of course she has." Coralie swats Diana away, having never doubted the fecundity of her mate. "Now unhand my loyal companion. I need her with me."

Without even so much as a token apology, no matter how disingenuous, Pet is granted a reprieve and is summarily released. Still petrified, she dashes into Coralie's open arms, seeking refuge in the comforting warmth of her nurturing breast.

"Darling, you're safe now." Coralie hugs her tight. "I won't let anyone take you away from me."

Once calm has been well enough restored—the other Mistresses retiring to the drawing room amidst Liora's avid protests—Pet glides a hand over the small feminine swell of Coralie's abdomen, envisioning the tiny miracle contained therein. Lacking permission to speak, she peers up at Coralie, her head cocked questioningly.

"It's real, my love." Coralie nods, holding her hand in place. "In a few short months, we'll welcome our first baby into the world. How does that make you feel? You've sired your first child and given me something very precious."

Pet doesn't need words to express how that makes her feel. She sinks deeper into Coralie's embrace and sighs contentedly, her prominent erection pressed between them.

Epilogue

EPILOGUE

Twenty years later ...

UNABLE TO SLEEP, NEGLIGEE-CLAD, HEAVILY PREGNANT Coralie sits at the head of the High Council dining table in the dead of night, the room bathed in pearly moonlight spilling in through the naked windows. At forty-eight, she's no less breathtakingly beautiful than she was in her youth, but age has brought the addition of a few creases beside her eyes, some laugh lines, and her jet black hair is now aided by a bottle.

Cutting through the serene silence, the padding of hurried feet heralds Pet's arrival. She appears in the open doorway fresh out of bed, wearing only one of Coralie's satin blouses, lopsided and hastily buttoned, barely protecting her modesty.

Palpably distraught from having woken alone, she breathes a sigh of relief to find Coralie safe and well.

"It's all right, my darling," Coralie calls out to her, assuaging her distress. "Come to me." She lays a hand on her round belly. "Your baby woke me, that's all. I came here to think."

Ten years her junior, thirty-eight-year-old Pet has yet to develop any gray in her hair, but she's undoubtedly matured. With her bangs grown out and her hair tied back in a braid, her pretty face no longer has anywhere to hide. Not that she ever wants to. Not anymore.

Concerned for the wellbeing of mother and unborn child, and eagerly awaiting the birth of her latest progeny, she pats her own flat stomach and points to Coralie, wondering if she's about to go into labor.

"Soon." Coralie beckons her closer. "Sit with me. It won't be long now."

Pet smothers a yawn, rubs her sleepy eyes, and kneels on the red velvet cushion at Coralie's feet, nuzzling and caressing her tummy.

"You're so attentive." Coralie guides her hand to feel the movement of their kicking baby. "Is it any wonder that I'm still so absolutely head over heels for you?"

Purring, Pet drops a loving kiss on Coralie's firm stomach, then presses her ear to the bump, listening to the sounds within, thoroughly enchanted by the miracle she helped to create.

"You've given me everything I could ever have hoped for. Do you know that? You should be very proud of yourself." Coralie runs her fingers through Pet's hair before settling on the nape of her neck, softly massaging her. "I'm the head of the High Council, and it's all because of you. You've sired more children than any other companion in our coven's history and helped me to secure the future of our kind for many years to come." She pauses. "So now how do you feel about retirement?"

Pet lifts her head, her brow furrowed, confused.

"My childbearing days are coming to an end," Coralie explains. "My reproductive obligation to the coven will soon be over." She loops a finger through the brass ring on Pet's collar and draws her forward. "So what do you think, my love?" She maneuvers Pet between her thighs. "Do you want to be free of your obligation also?" She brings her hands to Pet's neck, clasping her thick leather collar, toying with the buckle. "Do you want to be rid of this? And of ... that." She peeks down at Pet's augmentation. "Talk to me, Pet. What do you want?"

Taken aback, not at all knowing what to say, Pet remains silent.

"Nothing between us ever has to change," Coralie assures her. "Coven law doesn't preclude it." She bends to kiss Pet's furrowed brow. "You'll always be my darling little Pet."

Pet pries Coralie's hands from her collar. "And I'll always be your companion." She shuffles forward, her stiffening priapus seeking entry to Coralie's body. "Always."

About the Author

Keira Michelle Telford is an award-winning author with a love for the gruesome, the macabre, and the downright filthy. She writes historical and contemporary erotic sapphic romance, and other sapphic fiction.

Erotic Lesbian Romance
Cadence of My Heart
The Housemistress

Historical Lesbian Romance
The Ruin of Us
Quicunque Vult
Never Come to Rest

Short Stories
Hoar & Rime
Evonnia & the Maiden
Falling Hard

Futanari
All the Devils (short story)

Website: www.keiramichelle.com
Twitter: @km_telford
Facebook: www.facebook.com/keiramichelletelford
Goodreads: www.goodreads.com/keiramichelle
Amazon: www.amazon.com/author/keiramichelle

www.ingramcontent.com/pod-product-compliance
Lightning Source LLC
Chambersburg PA
CBHW070333130626
46556CB00007B/2839